Callie caught her breath,
unable to believe what she saw. . . .

Star stood on the trail. Her ears were pinned back; her silver-gray tail thrashed about. Her dark eyes swirled with anger. She neighed and stepped off the trail toward Pepper, the horse Callie was riding. All at once Pepper wheeled around and fled, galloping hard into the forest.

"Whoa!" Callie yelled. She glanced quickly over her shoulder. Star was chasing them. Callie pulled back on Pepper's reins. "Stop!"

Pepper slowed; then she bucked. The reins flew from Callie's hands. Pepper bucked once more, and for an impossible moment Callie sailed through the air. She wondered why Star would chase her. She wondered whether the horse still loved her. Then the world went black.

Phantom Rider

the Haunted Trail

by
Janni Lee Simner

A GLC Book

AN
APPLE
PAPERBACK

SCHOLASTIC INC.
New York   Toronto   London   Auckland   Sydney

For my sister and brother, Jolie and Bret

ISBN 0-590-67314-9

This book is a work of fiction. Names, characters, places, and incidents are products of the author's imagination or are used fictitiously. Any resemblance to actual events, locales, or persons, living or dead, is entirely coincidental.

12 11 10 9 8 7 6 5 4   6 7 8 9/9 0 1/0

Printed in the U.S.A.   40

First Scholastic printing, August 1996

Chapter One

The worst thing about normal horses was how slow you had to ride.

Callie sat on a mare named Pepper, walking in circles around a small corral. She worked to keep her back straight, her heels down, her legs loose at Pepper's sides. The setting sun cast long shadows on the dust beneath them. Pepper's speckled red coat glistened. Perched on a mesquite tree just outside the corral, a dove cooed. Behind Callie, somewhere among the stalls of Sonoran Stables, another bird answered, and the sound echoed through the hot July evening. Callie felt the heat against her arms. She smelled it in the dry, dusty air.

Josh Ryan, her riding instructor, stood watching from beneath the shade of the mesquite. A battered straw cowboy hat covered his head; dirty-blond hair spilled out beneath it and fell to his shoulders. Josh was the brother of Callie's friend Amy; they both lived right across the street from her.

"Turn left and cross the ring," Josh said.

1

Callie squeezed her right leg against Pepper's side, pushing the horse in the direction she wanted to go. Pepper ignored her. Callie squeezed harder. Still nothing. Finally she tugged lightly on the reins. Pepper sighed, turned, and slowly crossed the corral.

"All the way around the ring now," Josh said. "Don't let her cut across." Pepper cut across anyway. "Try that again. Heels down, toes up . . . much better. You're pretty comfortable on horseback for such a new rider."

But Callie wasn't really a new rider. That was the problem.

For the first month after her family had moved from New York to just outside Tucson, she had ridden secretly almost every night. She'd ridden a horse much more talented and sensitive than Pepper. A horse who always knew what Callie wanted, no matter how she handled her legs and the reins. A horse who understood Callie's thoughts and feelings, and whose thoughts and feelings Callie sometimes understood in return.

The horse's name was Star, and from the beginning Callie had known she was special, even magical. What Callie hadn't known until later was why Star was so unusual—because the beautiful, mysterious horse was actually a ghost.

Being a ghost meant Star had had an owner back when she was alive. His name was Michael, and he'd died when he was fourteen, in a mountain fire caused by a summer lightning strike. Star had died soon after. Callie shivered. Every time she thought about that fire, about the awful smell of Star's burning hair, about Michael lying so still on the ground, she got scared all over again. And Michael had been only a year older than Callie. Sometimes Callie thought that was the most frightening thing of all.

It was for Michael—or rather, Michael's ghost—that Star had eventually left Callie again. Callie knew that Star had needed to leave. She'd been the one who helped Star return to Michael. But even now, almost a month later, she still missed the horse.

"Are you with me?" Josh asked, breaking into Callie's thoughts.

"Yeah, I'm here," Callie said.

"Okay," Josh told her. "Try walking in a figure eight, then."

Callie thought of the moonlit nights when she and Star had run breathlessly through her yard together. She looked down at Pepper. Even regular horses didn't always just walk.

Callie squeezed Pepper with both legs. Pepper kept walking. Callie clicked with her tongue, but Pepper ignored that too. Frustrated, Callie kicked the horse as hard as she could.

Pepper bolted for the far side of the corral at a gallop. The gait was much rougher than Star's had ever been, and Callie fought to stay on Pepper's back. Clouds of dust flew up beneath the horse's hooves, getting into Callie's eyes and up her nose. The trees outside the corral flew by. Another moment and they'd crash into the fence. Callie pulled desperately back on the reins. Pepper skittered sideways; Callie almost fell. Finally the horse stopped, just inches short of the metal railing. Callie sat in the saddle, breathing hard.

She heard Josh yelling. He ducked under the fence and ran to her. "What are you trying to do?" he said. "Get yourself thrown?"

"I wouldn't have been thrown," Callie said sullenly, though she wasn't at all sure of that.

Josh stared at her a moment. He had the deepest blue eyes of anyone she knew. He took off his hat and hung it on one of the mesquite branches. "Why don't we just call it a day?" he said.

Callie nodded. She was tired of the lesson, anyway. She didn't feel like she was getting anywhere with her riding. She let Josh take the reins, then swung her leg over Pepper's back and jumped to the ground.

Pepper calmly nudged Callie's chest with her nose, as if she hadn't been out of control just a moment before. The horse's sides were slick with sweat, though. Callie wiped the sweat from her own forehead. Her hand brushed against her riding helmet. The hot plastic burned; she jerked her hand away.

Josh took a deep breath. Callie knew that sound from her own parents. She braced herself for a lecture.

Instead Josh said, "I know why you did that."

"You do?" Josh didn't know about Star, did he?

Josh ran a hand through his hair. "Sure. Learning to ride is slow, hard work. Sooner or later most new riders get impatient. Bored, even. Right?"

Callie nodded. Somehow she hadn't realized that other new riders—riders who'd never been on a horse like Star—might get frustrated, too.

"The thing is," Josh said, "I could let you gallop tomorrow, if all you cared about was going fast. But if you want to be a halfway decent rider—not to mention a safe one—you have to work at it a bit more. The question is, are you willing to do that?"

"Of course," Callie said. The only thing worse than not riding Star would be not riding at all. Besides, she really did love horses, even regular ones like Pepper. She'd always dreamed of riding, since long before she'd moved to Arizona. She wasn't about to give up on that dream now.

"Good," Josh said. "Because you're one of the more talented students I've taught in a while."

If she was talented, Callie didn't want to know what the really bad riders were like.

"So," Josh said, "what do you say next week we do something to break the routine?"

"Like what?" Anything was better than another week of walking in circles.

"I'm taking a couple of my other students on a trail ride up into the mountains next Monday," Josh said. "We're planning to start at sunrise, rest in the pine forest at Marshall Springs Campground during the hottest part of the day, then ride back through the late afternoon and early evening. That's about seven miles each way, but you're more than up to it. And there are some spectacular waterfalls near the campground itself. Interested?"

"A forest?" Callie asked. "Here?" She looked at the tall saguaro cacti and dry grass around her. She couldn't picture a forest anywhere within riding distance.

Josh grinned. "I take it you haven't been very far into the mountains yet. It's a whole other world up above six thousand feet."

"Sounds fun," Callie said. Josh was right; she really did need a break from her lessons.

"Hey," someone called, "when are you going to get around to asking me along on this ride?"

Callie looked up to see Amy Ryan walking toward them. Amy looked a lot like Josh: tall and lanky, but with black hair instead of blond, brown eyes instead of blue. She was right around Callie's age, and the two of them had spent a lot of time together since Callie had moved to Tucson.

"Oh, I don't know," Josh said with a lazy smile. "I thought maybe I'd just leave my kid sister home this time."

Amy put her hands on her hips. "I'm not a kid, and if I'm your sister, it's through no fault of my own."

Josh laughed. "Well, don't blame me. I was here first, you know."

"And that," Amy said, "isn't my fault either. Now, are you going to let Callie get out of the sun, or are you building heat endurance into her lessons today?"

"There's a thought," Josh said, but he handed the reins to Callie anyway. "Then again, I wouldn't want to miss my lesson with the Gareth twins, would I?"

Amy snickered. Callie had only seen the seven-year-old Gareth twins ride once. One of them had spent all her time cooing over how pretty her horse was and ignoring Josh. The other had pulled on her horse's mane or tail whenever she thought Josh wasn't looking.

"See you Monday?" Josh asked Callie. Callie nodded.

"Great," Josh said. "I'll touch base with your parents about the details later."

"Thanks for asking me," Callie said.

"Have fun with the Gareth twins," Amy told him. She started toward the stalls. Callie, leading Pepper by the reins, followed. The mare snorted, as if she too looked forward to riding outside the ring.

Callie led Pepper to her stall—which was nothing more than a rectangle of metal fence with a tin roof overhead. Winters in the Southwest were warm enough, Amy had explained once, that the horses didn't need anything fancier.

Winter felt ages away, though. Sweat trickled down Callie's face, and her arms were turning red in spite of all the sunscreen she'd put on before her lesson. She took off her riding helmet and replaced it with a floppy canvas hat she'd left in the stall. Like most Tucsonans, Callie had learned to stay indoors during the blazing hot summer afternoons. She had to get outside sometime, though. She'd go crazy if she didn't.

Amy followed Callie into the stall and closed the gate behind her. She wiped the sweat from her face. "I can't wait until it rains," she said.

Callie looked around. There were a few white clouds over the mountain peaks, but nothing more. "I was beginning to wonder if it ever rained here," she admitted.

Amy laughed. "Oh, when the rain comes

you'll know it. They don't call July and August monsoon season here for nothing."

Callie glanced at the clouds again. Then she went to Pepper's side, uncinched the saddle, and lifted it off the horse's back. The saddle was heavy, but after a few lessons Callie was getting used to the weight. Amy removed Pepper's bridle and saddle blanket. Together the two girls carried the tack to a wooden shed and set it down by some other saddles.

Callie grabbed a bucket full of grooming brushes, and they returned to Pepper's stall. Josh thought it was important for his students not only to be good riders but also to know how to take care of the horses. Callie didn't mind at all; she enjoyed grooming Pepper.

Callie took a currycomb out of the bucket and started brushing Pepper's red coat. The mare's sweat dripped to the ground. Pepper turned her head and nudged Callie's pocket.

"Do you think I have carrots there?" Callie asked.

Pepper snorted, as if that was a silly question. Callie reached into her jeans, pulled out a carrot, broke it in half, and gave the top to Pepper. Pepper chewed happily. Callie continued brushing.

"Pepper's a good horse to learn from," Amy said. "Most of the time she'll only do what you tell her to."

"Sometimes not even that much," Callie said, remembering how hard it had been to get Pepper to turn. She walked around to brush Pepper's other side.

"Bad lesson?" Amy asked.

Callie shrugged.

"You still miss Star, don't you?" Amy said.

"Yeah," Callie said. Amy was the only person she'd told about Star.

Callie set the currycomb down and pulled out a hoof pick. She reached for Pepper's front left hoof. Pepper, knowing what she wanted, lifted her hoof off the ground. Callie scraped dirt and pebbles away.

"I wish I could have met Star," Amy said. She'd been saying that ever since Callie had first told her about the ghost horse.

"I wish you could have, too," Callie said, though mostly she just wished she could see the horse again herself. She walked to Pepper's rear left hoof and picked the dirt away, then did the same for the hooves on Pepper's right side.

When she was through, Pepper nudged her pocket again. Callie laughed. "Oh, all right," she said. She gave Pepper the other half of the carrot, then looked around.

The sun had dipped below the horizon. A band of orange shone to the northwest; to the southwest the distant Tucson Mountains were purple against a pale blue sky. To the east, the jagged Catalina Mountains had turned from gray to deep red. The Catalinas were right behind the stables, and trails led deep into the mountains. Above their peaks, thin clouds glowed like molten gold. Before the move, Callie had never paid much attention to the sky, but Tucson sunsets were gorgeous.

"I'd better get home," Callie said. "You know how Dad feels about my being out after dark."

Amy shook her head. "Your family worries so much sometimes. I'd go crazy if Josh was like that." Josh was Amy's guardian, and had been ever since their parents were killed in a car crash a few years earlier.

"At least Mom and Dad are better than they used to be," Callie said. She and her parents used to fight a lot, but lately they'd managed to talk more and argue less.

"Too bad you can't say the same thing about your sister," Amy said.

"Tell me about it," Callie said. If anything, Melissa had been harder to get along with since they'd moved. Callie looked at the sky. The light was already fading. "I have to go."

"I'll walk with you," Amy said.

Callie put Pepper's grooming brushes away, and then she and Amy started for home.

11

Chapter Two

Callie and Amy lived less than a mile from the stables. Together they walked along the bottom of a sandy wash. Supposedly the washes were really riverbeds, but Callie had trouble believing that. She'd never seen any water in them, after all.

As they walked, Callie noticed a paperback book in Amy's back pocket. It looked like some sort of romance. Amy read anything she could get her hands on. Just over the past week Callie had seen her reading two mysteries, Homer's *Odyssey*, a book on edible plants of the Southwest, and a thriller that had something to do with rock climbing.

The wash led them to the far end of Callie's backyard. The yard was huge compared to her old house on Long Island, two acres in all. It was filled with scraggly cacti, uprooted weeds, rusted fences, and lots of dust. Callie had pulled up most of the weeds herself. She was helping her parents clean the yard in return for her riding lessons.

Off to one side of the yard was a circle of trampled dirt. When Star had been alive and the house had been part of a ranch, the circle had been a riding corral. Callie knew exactly what it used to look like; she'd seen it in dreams she'd had about Star and Michael.

Callie's dad was thinking of putting in a swimming pool where the corral used to be. Callie didn't know how she felt about that. She really wanted a pool—especially on days like this, when she came home all hot and dusty from riding—but she also hated losing what was left of the corral. She and Star had ridden there, after all.

Callie and Amy crossed the yard, walked around Callie's house, and said good-bye at her front door. Amy crossed the dirt road that separated their houses, pulling the book out of her pocket as soon as she reached the other side. Callie turned and hurried inside.

Melissa was in the living room, sprawled out in front of the television. She looked up when Callie walked in.

"You're late," Melissa said, sounding bored—with Callie or the TV show, Callie couldn't tell which. Melissa's skin was much paler than Callie's; red curls stood out against her white face. Unlike Callie, she'd hardly gone outside at all since arriving in Tucson. She always said it was too hot.

"It's not even eight yet." The air-conditioned air felt cold against Callie's sweaty skin. She shivered. Melissa glared at her, as if wondering how anyone could feel cold with so much heat outside.

"Well, some of us are getting hungry, you know. Dinner's been ready since before the last commercial."

"What are we eating?" Callie asked.

"Spinach soufflé," Melissa said, as if that were the most normal dinner in the world. Melissa never complained about the weird things Mom and Dad cooked.

"You should have started without me." Callie wrinkled her nose. "You should have finished without me, too."

Melissa rolled her eyes. "Really, Callie, there's no need to act so immature."

Callie bit back her response. She'd been trying not to argue with Melissa lately, but it wasn't easy. Melissa seemed to enjoy insulting Callie. She was always telling her she was just a kid— though Callie was almost thirteen, and Melissa was only two years older—and generally giving her a hard time. Sometimes Callie envied how well Josh and Amy got along. Maybe that was just because Josh was so much older than Amy. At any rate, Callie couldn't remember ever liking her sister.

She brushed past Melissa without another

word. Melissa stood, turned off the TV, and followed her into the kitchen.

Mom and Dad were already at the table. Mom's hair was the same deep red as Melissa's, with not a strand out of place. Dad, however, seemed tired; his hair and face were sweaty. Callie remembered that he'd been outdoors that day, examining a site for a new housing development being planned by his architecture firm. Mom was a computer programmer, so she worked indoors more than Dad did.

"Sorry I'm late," Callie told them as she walked in. She quickly washed her hands, then sat down.

Callie's father looked at her curiously. She could tell he wanted to know why she hadn't gotten home earlier. A month before, that probably would have started a fight between them.

"Sorry, Dad," Callie said again. "My lesson ran long, and then I still had to groom Pepper." She didn't tell him about the way she'd kicked the horse, or about Josh's talk with her afterward, which were the real things that had held her up. "Josh says it's irresponsible to leave a horse untended. I made sure I was home before dark, at least."

"Well, I appreciate that," Dad said. "No place is safe after dark these days. And of course I'm glad you take your responsibilities seriously." He spooned out some soufflé—it was bright green and oozed across his plate—and passed the dish around. "But try to get home earlier next time, okay?"

"Speaking of responsibilities," Mom said, "the yard is shaping up nicely. You've gotten a lot done in just a few weeks."

"I don't see how you can work in this heat, myself," Melissa said. She passed the soufflé to Callie.

Callie shrugged. If Amy and Josh were right, it'd be hot until October. Did her sister really plan to stay indoors until then?

Callie spooned out a thin layer of soufflé. She set the serving dish down and ate a tiny bite of the stuff. To her surprise, it wasn't bad; the taste of cheese was as strong as the taste of spinach. She ate another, larger bite, then spooned more onto her plate.

"Did you know there are forests up in the mountains?" she asked. "Josh is arranging a ride up there next week. He asked me if I wanted to come."

Melissa set down her fork and looked across the table, as if suddenly interested in what Callie was saying.

"A couple of Josh's other students are riding, too," Callie said. "And Amy. Can I go?" Callie bit her lip, hoping they'd agree. She'd already told Josh she was going, but there was always the chance her parents wouldn't give her permission. Parents could be funny like that. Callie had learned that the hard way.

But Mom just said, "That sounds fine with me, Callie. Josh seems pretty responsible, after all. I've been very impressed with the way he's raising Amy on his own."

"Great!" Callie said. "Thanks."

"I want to go with you," Melissa said abruptly.

"What?" Callie stared at her sister. The one time Melissa had gone on a trail ride—a short, one-hour ride with Callie, Amy, and Josh during her first week in Tucson—Melissa's horse had broken into a trot. Melissa had panicked and lost control of the animal. After that, she'd sworn she would never ride again. She'd almost convinced their parents not to let Callie ride, either.

"If you can go, then I should certainly be allowed to," Melissa said. Her voice was calm and reasonable. "I *am* older, after all."

"But you hate horses," Callie said. "And you hate going out in the heat."

Melissa shrugged. "Maybe I changed my mind."

Callie glared at her. Melissa just smiled sweetly. Callie hated when she did that. "Maybe you want to flirt with Josh," Callie said. She couldn't think of any other reason Melissa would ride again. Melissa had had a crush on Josh ever since they'd arrived in Tucson, even though he was almost ten years older than she was.

Callie kept glaring. If Melissa came along on the ride, she'd mess things up somehow. She always did.

"Callie, stop that," Dad said. Callie turned away from her sister and glared at her plate instead. "I really don't see what the problem is," Dad said. "When we agreed to let you take lessons, we said Melissa could ride as well if she wanted to."

"But Melissa's hardly ridden at all," Callie said. "She's not ready to ride all day! She'll get in the way!"

"How would you know what I can and can't do?" Melissa asked icily.

"I know a lot more about horses than you do," Callie said. "That's how."

"Callie, Melissa, please." Dad looked at them. "I assume you both can judge how long you're able to ride."

"But, Dad—"

"No *buts*," Dad said. "So long as it's okay with Josh, you can both go."

Callie sighed. She wanted to protest further, but she was afraid that if she did, her parents would decide not to let her go at all.

She turned back to her soufflé. She tried not to think about Melissa at all. Instead she thought about galloping horses and forests hidden in the middle of the desert.

Callie hoped Josh wouldn't let Melissa ride. She hoped he would decide she didn't have enough experience, or that there wasn't enough room for anyone else to come. She had no such luck. Instead, one of the other two students scheduled to ride canceled out; her parents wanted to escape the July heat and had rented a cabin up north for a few days. There was plenty of space for Melissa.

Josh did give Melissa a test lesson a few days before the ride. He explained the basics of how to handle a horse on the trail, and he reminded her that a day ride could be long and a little bit tiring. Then he agreed to let her go. "We'll put you on Butterscotch," he said. "He's a pretty mellow trail horse. You'll be fine."

By the day before the ride, a cool forest sounded good enough that Callie was almost willing to put up with Melissa. The desert was usually very dry—that was the only thing that made the heat bearable—but over the past few days the humidity had gone up, making the air damp and sticky. Small clouds hovered around the mountains. Amy kept muttering about wanting rain, but all the clouds did was add to some amazing sunsets.

The night before the ride, Callie dreamed about Star.

She dreamed they galloped together beneath a bright, full moon, through fields of dry summer grass. Star's silver-gray coat shimmered; the star-shaped blaze on her forehead shone brightly. Callie felt as though she and the horse were one creature, moving and thinking together. Around them, moonlight made the world silvery and magical. The mountains loomed ahead of them, purple-red in the light.

Callie's feet hung loose outside the stirrups; her hands didn't bother with the reins. Star knew what Callie wanted to do—when she wanted to turn, when she wanted to run faster—and did it. Callie sat tall and straight in the saddle, not bouncing no matter how hard they rode.

She'd never ridden this well, not on Star or any other horse. That should have been enough to tell her she was dreaming. But she just kept riding, as if it were the most natural thing in the world, as if Star had never left her.

After a long time, the moon set. A bird trilled in the distance. The silver and the magic fled, leaving only the gray light of dawn. Somehow Callie knew then that she really was dreaming. She also knew that this was an ordinary dream, different from the dreams she'd once had about Star's and Michael's past together. A weight like lead settled in her stomach. She didn't want to wake up.

Star's ears perked up, as if she heard a sound. Abruptly the mare stopped running and stood still, listening. Callie listened as well but didn't hear anything unusual. She followed Star's gaze, but she didn't see anything, either.

She felt Star's restlessness, though. Callie sighed and ran a hand along Star's silky neck. Then she swung from Star's back to the ground. Star lifted her head, snorted, and quickly galloped away. Callie stared after the horse, watching Star leave her once more. As she watched, the dream began to dissolve. The fields around her grew hazy and indistinct.

Callie awoke alone, in the darkness of her own room.

Chapter Three

Callie jumped out of bed, ran to her window, and threw it open. Damp night air flooded the room. She looked outside.

Star was nowhere in sight. Callie hadn't really expected her to be, but she couldn't help looking, just in case.

She'd had lots of dreams about Star since the horse left her. After every one of them she'd run to the window, and after every one she'd found the same empty yard.

The night was black, and stars glittered nearly all the way down to the horizon. A dog or a coyote, Callie couldn't tell which, barked over and over again. For just a moment Callie had the odd feeling that someone was watching her from somewhere in the yard; then that too faded.

Callie bit back her disappointment. Star was gone. The sooner she stopped hoping the horse would return, the better.

She turned to look at her alarm clock—3:50 A.M., it said. They were supposed to meet Josh and Amy at five. That way they could start riding at dawn, before the heat set in. There was no point in going back to sleep now. She grabbed a pair of jeans and a T-shirt and went into the shower instead.

Within fifteen minutes Callie was dressed and ready to ride. An hour later Melissa was still in the bathroom, fighting with her curling iron and muttering that it was too early to be awake.

Callie filled some old camping canteens with water. Her family had camped only once, years ago, and no one but Callie had enjoyed it. They still had all their old equipment, though.

She'd already made sandwiches for her and Melissa while she was waiting, as well as getting together fruit and trail mix to munch on along the way. She packed the food and water in an old backpack. She slathered sunscreen on her arms and face, then added that to the supplies. Finally she set the backpack down by the front door. Once they got to the stables, they'd repack everything on the horses.

Callie put on her hat and went to the bathroom to check on Melissa. Her sister had finished curling her hair; now she was fiddling with lipstick and eye shadow.

"What do you need makeup for?" Callie asked. Did Melissa really expect Josh to be impressed by that stuff? "You'll only sweat it off once the sun comes up."

Melissa rolled her eyes. "You don't expect me to go out looking like a slob, do you?" She pursed her lips, dabbed off some extra lipstick, and turned to Callie. "That hat looks really weird," Melissa said. "Can't you find something more flattering?"

Callie gritted her teeth. She wished Melissa would just stay home. "The hat will keep off the sun," Callie snapped. "That's all that really matters."

"To you, maybe." Melissa squinted at the mirror as she applied some mascara. Her hand slipped; the mascara left a dark mark on her cheek. Melissa sighed and washed it away.

Dad walked by and told the girls he was going out to start the car. Josh had offered to drive them over, but he'd needed to leave earlier to saddle up the horses, and even Callie hadn't been willing to head out much before five.

"I hate mornings," Melissa muttered. "And I hate morning people. Since when are you up so early, anyway? A few weeks ago you wouldn't get out of bed before noon."

Callie didn't answer. The reason she'd slept so late was because of Star. After staying out all night riding, she'd needed to catch up on her sleep.

Melissa stared at Callie. Melissa didn't know about Star, but she had caught Callie sneaking

24

out late at night. Callie avoided her sister's gaze and looked down at her feet instead.

"You know I don't believe those excuses you gave Mom and Dad," Melissa said. "One of these days I'm going to find out what really happened." She turned back to the mirror.

Melissa finished putting on her makeup and ran a brush through her hair. "There," she said. "How do I look?"

Callie looked at her sister. Melissa wore snug jeans, a purple tank top, and black suede boots. Callie glanced down at her own battered jeans and worn sneakers. "You look fine, I guess," Callie said. "If you're going to a party. Doesn't look very comfortable for riding, though."

"So?" Melissa said. "There are more important things than being comfortable." She walked past Callie and out of the bathroom. "Are you coming?" she called from the front door. "We don't want to be late."

"I'm not the one who was holding us up," Callie called after her. She grabbed the backpack and followed her sister outside.

The night had given way to thin gray light. The relatively cool morning air felt wonderful. In summer the best part of the desert day was before the sun came up.

Dad had the car engine running. Melissa climbed into the front seat; Callie sat in the back. She would have been just as happy to walk, but Dad's no-walking-after-dark rule seemed to apply early in the morning as well as at night. Besides, Melissa claimed her boots were too tight to walk very far in.

"How do you expect to ride in shoes you can't even walk in?" Callie asked as they drove.

Melissa just shook her head. "Don't you understand *anything?*"

"I sure don't understand you," Callie muttered.

Dad glanced over at them. "Both of you stop it, all right?"

They drove the rest of the way to the stables in silence.

Josh and Amy were waiting for them. They both wore jeans and cowboy boots. Unlike Melissa's, their boots were battered and scuffed, clearly boots that had been worked in. Josh wore a long-sleeved work shirt and a straw hat; Amy wore a T-shirt and her white plastic riding helmet. A light jacket was knotted around her waist. Callie couldn't imagine wanting a jacket, not even in the relatively cool morning, but Amy had grown up in Tucson. The weather felt normal to her.

Four horses were already saddled and tied to a nearby fence; Pepper was among them. A pair of canvas saddlebags was slung behind each saddle.

"Shouldn't there be five horses?" Callie asked.

"Brian had to cancel," Josh told her. Callie guessed Brian was the other student. "His mom called last night and said he wasn't feeling well. It's just us."

"Josh's boss wanted to cancel the whole ride," Amy said. "She always complains she doesn't make enough money off small rides. Josh talked her out of it, though."

Josh laughed. "That's just because I knew Amy would nag me forever if we didn't go."

"Who, me?" Amy smiled innocently. Josh laughed louder.

Amy started toward the horses, and Callie followed her. Together they redistributed the supplies in Callie's backpack to a couple of the saddlebags. There were already some apples and carrots packed in them—snacks for the horses and humans both, Amy said. Two of the canteens they set aside, tying them to the saddle horns so they'd be within reach during the ride.

When they were through, Callie and Amy wandered back to the car, where Dad was filling out some paperwork Josh had given him. Sonoran Stables always required a release form before anyone rode their horses, and the form they used for trail rides was slightly different from the one they used for

lessons. Mostly, both forms said you understood that horses were sometimes unpredict-
able and you wouldn't hold the stables liable
for any injuries.

Dad read the form over, wrote in Callie's and
Melissa's names, and signed it. He gave the
form and money for the ride to Josh, hugged
the girls, and drove off.

Josh went to the office to get riding helmets
for Callie and Melissa. A light was on in the
office building, and nearby, one of the other
stable employees carted a wheelbarrow full of
hay to the other horses for breakfast.

Josh returned with the helmets. Callie folded
her hat up and put it into a saddlebag; she
might want it later when they stopped to rest
and have lunch. Then she strapped on the helmet. She'd fallen often enough around Star that
she never argued about wearing one.

Melissa looked at her helmet skeptically.
"Do you really think this is necessary?" she
asked. After the way Melissa had panicked on
their last ride, Callie would have expected her
to be glad to wear a helmet. Was Melissa afraid
the helmet would mess up her hair?

"Yeah, it's needed," Josh said. "Especially
since your dad didn't sign the line waiving the
helmet requirement. I prefer to see new riders
wear them, anyway."

"Well, if you think it's important, of course

I'll wear a helmet." Melissa smiled at Josh, her eyes so large and syrupy Callie nearly gagged. Josh kind of looked at her for a moment, then raised one eyebrow and turned toward the horses. Callie heard Amy's muffled giggling.

"Okay," Josh said, "let's ride."

Callie automatically went to Pepper's side. Pepper snorted; Callie scratched the mare behind the ears. Pepper dropped her head and nudged Callie's pocket.

"Sorry," Callie said. "The carrots are packed in the saddlebags this time." Pepper let out a heaving sigh. Callie laughed.

She untied Pepper's lead rope from the fence, unlatched it from her bridle, and stashed it in a saddlebag. Then she stepped into Pepper's left stirrup, grabbed the mare's mane, and swung onto her back.

Callie looked around at the stables, at the other horses, at the gray mountains. No matter how much she rode, she never got tired of seeing the world from horseback, of feeling so incredibly tall.

Amy rode up beside Callie. She sat straight in the saddle, completely at ease. She was on a tall deep brown horse with a black mane and tail. In spite of his height—or maybe because of it—Amy's horse was named Tiny. Horses with his coloring were called bay horses. Pepper, on the other hand, was a chestnut roan.

Star had been a gray, though she'd more often looked silver to Callie.

Nearby, Josh helped Melissa onto Butterscotch, a cream gelding. Once she was in the saddle, Melissa smiled brightly and thanked Josh. Josh just shrugged and walked over to his horse, a chestnut gelding named Rusty. Even though Josh boarded him at the stables, Rusty was Josh's own horse, and had been for several years.

Josh jumped onto Rusty's back in one quick motion. He looked completely natural in the saddle, as if he'd been born there. He squeezed his legs slightly, and Rusty started walking. The other horses fell into place behind him: first Butterscotch with Melissa, then Pepper with Callie, then Tiny with Amy bringing up the rear.

The horses followed a wide dirt road to a narrower trail. At the start of the trail, Callie saw a small sign: ENTERING CORONADO NATIONAL FOREST. Most of the Catalina Mountains were national forest land; that was why few people lived there. There were one or two small towns, but the rest of the mountains had been set aside as a wilderness area.

The horses followed the trail uphill, into the beginning of the mountains. The trail wound back and forth as it rose, crossing a dry, rocky wash several times. The air smelled dusty, like the desert always smelled, though a little bit damper on account of the humidity. Pepper lifted her head up, as if sniffing the air. Her steps were perkier now that they'd left the stables, much more energetic than during Callie's lessons. Pepper seemed as excited about riding as Callie was. She was much more enthusiastic than the horse Callie had ridden on her last trail ride; that horse had hardly wanted to move at all.

Cacti of just about every kind were around them—spiky pincushions, fuzzy cholla, paddle-shaped prickly pear, tall branched saguaro. Once, Pepper leaned her head down toward the cholla, sniffing curiously. Callie pulled her quickly away. Probably Pepper had enough sense not to get too close, but Callie didn't want to take any chances on her getting a faceful of stickers. Pepper sighed dramatically—horses were so good at that—and kept walking.

Chalky green creosote bushes were everywhere, as well as a few green-barked palo verde and gnarled mesquite trees. There were some ocotillo along the trail, too, which shed their leaves in dry weather and looked like little more than dead gray sticks now.

After a while the gray dawn gave way to pink light. Birds chirped loudly, as if calling for the sun to come up—or, more likely, taking advantage of the cool before sunrise. The trail veered left, away from the wash, and climbed more steeply uphill. Pepper slowed down, carefully picking her way among the rocks. Callie leaned forward to keep her balance. Pepper felt strong and steady beneath her; Callie reached out and patted the horse's shoulder.

A wall of rock rose to their left; a few yards to the right, the wash dropped quickly away. Soon the horses were climbing the wall of a canyon. Callie looked across the chasm to where another, even taller rock wall rose above the wash. Far ahead of her she saw jagged mountain peaks. Yellow light shone like an aura above them.

Without warning, the sun poked over the mountains. All at once the air turned to shimmering gold. Pepper's chestnut coat glistened in the light—not the way Star's coat used to glow, but magical nonetheless. Callie kept riding, surrounded by beauty, feeling Pepper's steady gait beneath her. For once she didn't have to worry about how well she was balanced in the saddle, or where her legs were, or how crisply she executed her turns.

For the first time since Star had left, Callie was riding entirely for the joy of riding.

Pepper slipped on a rock; it slid out from beneath her hoof, bounced away, and fell down into the canyon. The horse's ears went back, but Callie patted her reassuringly, and the mare quickly regained her footing.

Melissa glanced back at Callie. She looked nervously into the canyon, then at the rocks beneath Butterscotch's feet. Her hand clutched the reins a little more tightly. "Are you sure this is safe?" she asked Josh.

"Just trust your horse," Josh called back. "Butterscotch knows this trail forward and backward, and probably upside down, too."

"Of course he does," Melissa said, but she looked uneasy.

Callie looked down at Pepper's feet. She could almost see Pepper thinking: hesitating when she reached a particularly steep part of the trail, examining the rocks and considering where to put her hooves, then stepping ahead. Like Josh said, the horses knew what they were doing.

As they climbed the canyon the landscape changed. The cacti grew sparser. The canyon floor below them rose, until the chasm wasn't nearly as deep as before. Then, without warning, the canyon disappeared. The trail leveled out, and they emerged into a grassy basin. To their right, several hundred yards away, the wash cut through the tall grass.

Grass was everywhere. Callie pulled up on Pepper's reins to keep her from munching on it. The cacti were just about gone now, and there were more and more trees along the trail. The new trees had leaves that were darker green than any Callie had seen since moving to the desert. They were almost like the trees back in New York, though shorter and bushier. A few even had what looked like miniature oak leaves.

Callie looked out over the grassland, toward the still-distant mountain peaks. She squinted; the sun, now all the way over the peaks, was very bright. Small white clouds—the same sort she'd seen all week—hovered over the mountains. The day was warming up, though it wasn't hot yet.

A brownish-gray gecko darted across the trail. Pepper's ears twitched, but she kept walking. A moment later something gray and fuzzy scrambled by in the other direction. Callie watched the animal scurry up into the branches of a tree.

"It's a squirrel!" She laughed. She realized she hadn't seen a single squirrel since she'd moved to the desert.

From behind her Amy called, "Aren't there supposed to be lots of squirrels out East?"

"Tons of them," Callie agreed. "Mom used to complain they dug up the garden."

"That's what I'd read," Amy said. "But I thought maybe the book was exaggerating.

There are so few of them here, and they're mostly in the mountains."

Callie blinked. "You mean squirrels are as rare out here as lizards are out East?"

"Yeah," Amy said. "I guess so."

"It's just a squirrel," Melissa said. She turned to face them. "I don't see what the big deal is." She turned back to the trail. Callie glared at the back of her sister's head. Couldn't she even talk to her friend without Melissa getting in the way?

Without warning Melissa's horse stopped short, ears flat against his head. Pepper sidled away, giving Butterscotch more room.

"Whoa, girl." Callie patted Pepper's neck. "Take it easy." Pepper stopped.

Butterscotch turned his head about, ears pricking every which way, as if trying to figure out where some troubling sound had come from.

"Come on," Melissa said impatiently. She gave Butterscotch a sharp kick. Butterscotch nickered and reared up, kicking his front legs into the air. Melissa screamed, dropping the reins and clutching the saddle horn with both hands. Callie caught her breath.

Josh pulled Rusty to a stop, jumped from his back, and ran toward Melissa.

"Quit it!" Melissa yelled. Butterscotch's feet

hit the ground again. He began skittering backward. Pepper twitched uneasily as the horse approached her.

Josh grabbed Butterscotch's reins; the horse stopped at once. Josh looked him straight in the eyes. "Stop that," he said. "Behave." Butterscotch stood stone still and stared at Josh, as if waiting for his next command.

Melissa took several deep, choking breaths. Her face was completely pale, and for just a second she looked as if she was about to burst into tears. But then she swallowed and instead of crying managed a forced smile.

Josh turned to Melissa. "Now then," he said, "what happened?"

Melissa told him; Josh listened, then turned and stared at Butterscotch thoughtfully. "Something spook you, boy? You're usually one of the calm ones." He looked back up at Melissa. "Sounds like he caught sight of something that scared him. He wanted to listen when you told him to go on ahead, but he was afraid to. Rearing back was sort of a compromise." Josh laughed. "The kind of compromise that only makes sense to a horse, of course."

"Of course," Melissa said, smiling weakly.

"As a general rule," Josh continued, "when your horse gets nervous like that, it's best to try to figure out what's spooking him before pushing on ahead."

"But nothing was wrong," Melissa said. "There's nothing frightening here."

"That's horse sense for you," Josh said. "Things that seem perfectly normal to you and me—a rustling tree branch, a rock that catches the sun at the wrong angle—can scare a horse right out of his skin sometimes."

"And a skinless horse isn't a pretty sight," Amy said. A grin tugged at the corners of her mouth. "You can't saddle them up, blood gets all over the place—"

"That's gross," Melissa said.

"It's just a joke," Callie told her.

Melissa ignored Callie. "How am I supposed to know when a horse is spooked and when he just wants to munch on the trees?" she asked Josh. "These horses stop all the time."

"That," Josh said, "takes experience." He turned from them without another word and mounted Rusty again.

Callie heard Melissa mutter under her breath, "How can I get experience if my stupid horse won't listen?"

Josh clicked his tongue; Rusty started forward. Butterscotch hesitated, ears still twitching. Hesitantly, Melissa kicked him. Butterscotch started walking, but he still seemed nervous and twitchy. Melissa was nervous, too. Her hands shook as she held the reins.

Pepper didn't follow. Callie squeezed her legs

and clicked her tongue, but the mare wouldn't move. Remembering Josh's words to Melissa, Callie followed Pepper's gaze, trying to figure out why the horse hesitated.

For just a moment she saw something: a glimmer of silver, half hidden by the trees and tall grass. A familiar tingling ran up and down her spine—the same tingling she used to feel when Star appeared.

When Callie tried to get a better look, the glimmer and the tingling both disappeared. Pepper started walking again.

Callie sighed. It was bad enough that she had to dream about Star. The last thing she needed was to start imagining she saw the horse, too. Star was gone. Why was it so hard to accept that?

Callie fixed her eyes firmly on the trail. She didn't let herself look back again, no matter how much she wanted to.

Chapter Four

As the horses continued through the grass, they still seemed uneasy. Pepper kept stamping her hooves, flicking her ears, and turning her head at imagined noises. Once, she threw her head back and nickered loudly, as if warning something away—or, perhaps, just warning the other horses to be careful. Over and over again Callie too thought she heard rustling in the trees. She didn't see Star again, though. She told herself that she didn't really expect to.

Maybe she was just picking up on the horses' nervousness. Maybe that was why she kept hearing things.

The day grew hot, though not as scalding as it would have been down in the valley. The trees grew larger and more frequent. Almost three hours into the ride, the trail veered right, leading them toward the wash. Callie smelled water. To her surprise, when they reached the wash it wasn't dry anymore. A small stream trickled through it. Around the water the trees were thicker than anywhere else.

Josh stopped at the stream and declared it was time for a break and a snack. Callie hoped the horses would settle down by the time they were ready to leave again.

Callie jumped out of the saddle, gave Pepper a reassuring pat, and pulled her lead rope out of the saddlebag.

"Here," Amy said, walking up beside her. "I'll show you where you can tie her." Together, they led their horses to the stream and tied them to the branches of a couple of the funny short oak trees. The horses stretched their necks down to the water and drank noisily.

"Horses," Amy laughed. "No manners at all."

"It's about time we stopped," Melissa said, walking up to them. She took a large bite out of an apple. "I'm famished. And tired."

"Um, aren't you leaving something behind?" Amy asked.

Melissa took another bite. "Like what?"

"Like your horse!" Amy pointed back to the trail, where Butterscotch stood loose, chewing on a leafy tree branch.

Melissa shrugged. "I'll get him in a minute," she said. "He's not going anywhere."

Amy's face turned red. Callie had never seen her friend so angry. "No, you'll get him now!" Amy said. "You always take care of your horse first, no matter how hungry you are. They're the ones doing most of the work, after all."

Amy started toward Butterscotch herself, but Josh, leading Rusty, was already headed that way. He grabbed Butterscotch's reins and led both horses to them.

"Forget something?" He handed the reins to Melissa. Unlike Amy, he looked more amused than annoyed. Melissa's cheeks turned scarlet, though. She grabbed the reins and didn't say another word as she tied her horse up by the stream.

Amy pulled a hoof pick out of her saddlebag and checked all the horses' feet to make sure they didn't have any small rocks caught in them. At Josh's suggestion, Callie went around and made sure all their saddles were still tightly cinched. When Callie and Amy were through, they gave the horses pieces of apple. All four animals chewed loudly, quickly finishing the apples. They turned to grazing on the grass.

"Now," Amy said, looking at Melissa, "we can get something to eat for ourselves."

They found a shaded spot beside the stream, one where they could keep an eye on the horses. The water wasn't drinkable for humans, but Callie splashed it on her face and arms. A light breeze evaporated the water and left her skin wonderfully cool.

She took a long drink from her canteen, then leaned back, closed her eyes, and listened to the water trickling by. A bird chirped irritably from the tree above her; some unknown animal rustled through the brush below. The animals were much quieter at midday than they had been at dawn.

Callie heard a sound, as if someone—a human, not a horse—was breathing right over her shoulder. She jumped up and looked around. No one was there. She shook her head. What was wrong with her? She hoped the horses were settling down better than she was.

Callie sat back down, took another drink of water, and reached for a handful of trail mix. "Hey," she said, looking at the mixture in her hand, "this stuff isn't all that different from the oats the horses eat back at the stables."

Amy laughed. "Yeah. We even eat it for the same reasons. It's a way to get lots of energy fast."

Josh grinned. "Of course, you're also welcome to graze on the grass while we're on the trail."

"Gee, thanks," Amy said.

"Only trying to be helpful," Josh said. He stood, stretching his long legs. "Five or ten more minutes, I think, and then we'll hit the trail again."

Callie got to her feet. Her legs were stiff after the short rest. She decided to walk the soreness out of them before getting back on horseback.

She wandered away from the trail, uphill a short way. Beyond some trees she saw what looked like an old wall. She walked up to it for a closer look. The wall, now crumbling away, was man-made, rocks placed deliberately one on top of another.

"Cool, isn't it?" Amy walked up behind her. "I'd almost forgotten this was here. It's part of some old house. I'm not sure who it belonged to. Probably an old homesteader."

Callie stared at the wall. She tried to imagine it as part of a house. She tried to imagine people living there, in the wilderness, unaware that one day strangers would hike through their home. She shivered. Would someone hike through the ruins of her house one day, too, and wonder who had lived there?

As if in response, she heard footsteps right behind her. Callie whirled around. The footsteps cut off abruptly. Were there hikers on the trail, too? Callie saw Josh and Melissa talking down by the stream, but otherwise no one was there. Callie looked a moment more—she knew she'd heard something—but she still didn't see anyone.

She turned back to the wall and looked beyond the rocks, wondering if there were any other signs of the homestead. Instead she saw something else—a shimmering silver horse, walking slowly through the grass. Could it really be Star? The sound of hooves was very different from the footsteps she'd heard just before.

Callie stepped forward, hoping that somehow the vision was real. A gust of wind blew; for a moment swaying branches blocked her view. When the wind died down, the shimmering image was gone. Callie blinked, fighting tears.

"What's wrong?" Amy asked.

Before Callie could answer, she heard a noise behind her again. When she turned around, though, she saw only Melissa, walking up to them.

"I want to talk to you guys," Melissa said. Her bare shoulders were pink from the sun. Hadn't she at least remembered to put on sunscreen? "I'm getting tired. I think we need to turn around."

"What?" Callie stared at her sister. How could Melissa want to turn back? They'd only been riding a few hours. They weren't anywhere near Marshall Springs Campground yet. Callie still wanted to see the forest and the waterfall. "We've barely gotten started," Callie said. "Why'd you come in the first place if you didn't really want to ride? You said you could handle it!"

"I didn't know I'd get tired this soon." Melissa's voice was so calm and reasonable that Callie wanted to scream. "Besides, my legs hurt."

"Three hours can be a pretty long time for someone without much experience," Amy admitted, though she too looked reluctant to turn back. "And we still have to ride out, too."

"Great!" Melissa said. Her face brightened. "Then you guys will tell Josh you want to turn around?"

"Us?" Callie said. "You're the one who wants to go home."

Melissa looked down at her fingernails. They were newly polished; Melissa must have found time to do that before leaving the house, too— or maybe she'd done them the night before. "Really, Callie," Melissa said, her voice taking on an edge Callie hated, "this whole ride was your idea. I think it's your responsibility to end it."

"No!" Anger made Callie's face hot. "If you want to go home, you can ask Josh yourself, and he can decide one way or the other." Callie had the sinking feeling that Josh would agree, though. Melissa had ruined things—again.

"Callie!" Melissa's tone was suddenly pleading. "Come on. I can't ask. It'd be embarrassing!"

"Why?" Amy shook her head, seeming genuinely confused. "There's nothing embarrassing about being tired. Josh will understand."

Melissa's face turned bright red. "You're the ones who don't understand!" She whirled away and ran from them.

Callie sighed. She started back toward the trail, Amy beside her.

When they arrived, they found Melissa already on her horse. She wasn't facing toward home, though. She was facing toward the stream—and farther into the mountains.

They wouldn't have to turn around after all.

Melissa had a strange, determined look on her face, and she refused to look at Callie. She must have decided not to say anything to Josh. Callie didn't really understand that—if she had been the one who wanted to go home, she would have just said so—but she wasn't about to argue. She hurried over to her horse. She didn't want to give Melissa any time to change her mind.

Callie repacked the saddlebags, untied Pepper, and jumped up onto the horse. Josh and Amy mounted Rusty and Tiny, and soon they were riding again. The horses still seemed a little bit unsettled, but they were much calmer than they had been.

The horses crossed the stream, splashing noisily. Water splattered into Pepper's face. She snorted and shook her head, spraying water all around her. Callie laughed.

For a few hundred yards the horses continued away from the stream. Then Josh turned, and they rode parallel to it. The trail sloped uphill again, though not as steeply as before.

The trees grew thicker and taller. The stream dipped out of sight to their left, and the sound of running water turned to a distant roar echoing off rock walls Callie couldn't see. Pepper's ears perked up as she listened to the sound. To their right the ground sloped upward. Beyond the trees Callie saw more mountain peaks.

The tall grass gave way to soft dirt and underbrush. Roots crossed the trail more and more often, and Pepper stepped carefully over them. Pines grew among the shorter trees, and when Callie looked down, she saw pine needles and old leaves along the trail. The horses continued forward. Underbrush crunched beneath their hooves.

The pines grew denser, stretching toward the sky and blocking the bright sun. Patches of blue sky, white cloud, and distant mountain showed between their branches. A cool breeze blew through the pine needles with a low roar surprisingly similar to the sound of the running stream. The breeze blew Pepper's mane gently about. A sweet smell of green leaves filled the air, along with the scent of rich earth. Callie inhaled deeply. She reached out and patted Pepper on the neck, wondering if the mare also appreciated the wonderful smell.

They were really in a forest, just like Josh had said they would be. Callie glanced at her watch; it was only a little after ten. She looked around, unable to believe she'd been surrounded by desert only five hours before. She loved the desert, but it felt good to be around real trees again, too. The desert's beauty was stark, bright, and stunning. The forest's beauty was softer and more comforting. Callie took another deep breath.

Without warning, Rusty threw his head back and nickered. He began to back wildly down the trail, feet sliding on dirt and pine needles. Butterscotch started backing up as well. Pepper's ears went back. Callie nudged Pepper with her leg, then tugged lightly on the reins. Pepper moved off the trail to the right, out of the way of the other horses. The mare's ears went flat against her head; her whole body was tense. Out of the corner of her eye, Callie saw Amy and Tiny edge off the trail in the other direction.

Melissa started yelling, demanding that someone get the horses under control. Callie stared at Rusty and Butterscotch. What were they scared of now? She didn't see anything but the trail and the trees.

Her spine tingled. The tingling spread to her arms and legs. She felt as though her whole body were falling asleep. She stared harder. There was something strange about the trail ahead of the horses. Both the ground and the air seemed indistinct, wavering as if Callie were seeing them through water. She squinted for a better look.

All at once the world snapped into focus. Callie caught her breath, unable to believe what she saw.

Star stood on the trail. This time Callie wasn't imagining it. Star's ears were pinned back; her silver-gray tail thrashed about. Her dark eyes swirled with anger. Callie felt that anger somewhere inside her, as strongly as if she were the one who was upset.

Pepper neighed. Star neighed back, a challenge in her voice.

Why was Star angry? That didn't make any sense. Her anger didn't make her any less beautiful, though; she had a fiery grace that took Callie's breath away. Even though Callie thought about Star all the time, in the month they'd been apart she'd forgotten just how stunning the horse really was. Star's silver-gray coat glimmered more brightly than Callie had remembered; the curve of her long neck was more graceful; the white mark on her forehead shone more brightly. Callie wanted to run to the horse, to hug her, to make the anger go away.

Star neighed again. She stepped off the trail, toward Pepper. Pepper backed nervously away. Star took another step. All at once Pepper wheeled around and fled, galloping hard into the forest.

"Whoa!" Callie yelled. She pulled back on Pepper's reins. "Stop!" Pepper galloped faster. Back by the trail, Callie heard the other horses whinnying and running, too. Someone screamed; she couldn't tell who. She heard hooves behind her and glanced quickly over her shoulder. Star was chasing them, nickering as she ran.

Callie kept pulling on Pepper's reins, but it didn't do any good. She heard Star close the gap between them. For a moment Pepper slowed; then she bucked. She kicked her legs wildly out behind her, then bucked again.

The reins flew from Callie's hands. Pepper bucked once more, and Callie flew out of the saddle. For an impossible moment she sailed through the air; then she crashed to the ground. Pain shot through her shoulder. She wondered why Star would chase her. She wondered whether the horse still loved her. Then the world went black.

Callie woke to a strange sound—somewhere between a rapid ticking and a hiss.

Someone gripped her arm, hard. "Don't move," Josh whispered. His voice was tense.

Fear trickled down Callie's spine. What was Josh scared of? She opened her eyes. Above her, beyond the pine branches, the sky was deep blue. The white clouds were piled around the mountain peaks, larger and thicker than before.

The ticking sound continued. Callie looked toward her feet.

A long brown snake with a diamond pattern on its back slowly uncoiled. Then, just as slowly, it slithered past her, disappearing among the rocks a few feet away. Josh let out a breath. He released his hold on Callie's arm.

Callie started trembling. "Was that a rattlesnake?"

Josh nodded. "Usually they're not very interested in people. Given half a chance, they'll run away rather than strike. But that one was awfully close." Josh ran a hand through his hair. His clothes were covered with dirt and pine needles; his hat was gone. "Can you stand?" he asked abruptly.

Callie sat up, then stood. For a moment her legs wobbled. She grabbed Josh's arm for support. The world steadied beneath her. Her shoulder hurt; she rolled the sleeve of her T-shirt back and saw the beginnings of a bruise. She stretched the arm out, wincing. It ached, but she could move it easily enough.

Josh examined the bruise. "It doesn't look broken," he said. "Though it may be sore for a while. You must have landed on your shoulder, then rolled over onto your back. Good thing you had those pine needles to cushion your fall."

Josh brushed a hand across his forehead. For the first time, Callie realized how stressed he looked. "I don't think I've ever been so glad I make people wear helmets," he said. A wry grin crossed his face, and he rubbed the side of his head. "Too bad I don't have the sense to follow my own advice. If I hadn't known when to jump . . ." His voice trailed off.

"You fell, too?"

"Everyone fell." Josh looked surprised she didn't know. "I saw a second rattler near the trail, which is unusual enough. That must be what spooked the horses." Josh didn't seem convinced, though. He shook his head. "Or maybe it was something else, something we humans wouldn't blink twice at. All I know is that I've never seen those horses so crazed. I just don't know what got into them. I've never lost a horse before, let alone four at once."

For a confused moment Callie wondered why Josh didn't know Star had spooked the horses. Then she remembered that no one but she could see Star. No human, that was. The horses had seen Star clearly enough. Could all horses see ghosts? Maybe that was why they spooked so easily.

She bit her lip, remembering how Star had chased her. Why had she done that? Didn't she care about Callie anymore? Callie fought not to cry.

"Are you okay?" Josh asked. "It's easy to get shaken up after a fall."

Callie shook her head. "I'm fine," she said. She looked around. "Where are the horses?" Neither Star nor the others were anywhere in sight.

"They're gone," Josh said.

"What do you mean, gone?" Normal horses didn't just disappear.

"Whatever spooked them scared them so badly that they ran away," Josh said. His voice was calm, but he looked more and more worried as he talked. He shoved his hands into his pockets. "I sure hope they're okay. As soon as I know everyone's all right, we'll look for them."

"I'm fine," Callie said. "Let's start looking." If the horses were frightened, she wanted to help calm them. It was the least she could do, after Star had scared them like that. She started toward the trail. She already felt much steadier, though her shoulder still hurt a little.

Someone screamed. Callie recognized Melissa's voice. Her veins turned to ice. Melissa screamed again.

Callie and Josh took off for the trail at a run.

Chapter Five

They found Melissa and Amy in a small clearing on the other side of the trail. Melissa lay on the ground. Her face was pale, but otherwise she seemed all right. She was glaring at Amy, who knelt beside her, hands around her left boot.

"That boot has to come off," Amy said. She looked up at Josh. "I think her ankle might be broken," she explained.

"Just leave me alone," Melissa said. She pulled her foot angrily away from Amy.

"Amy's only trying to help," Callie said.

Josh knelt by Melissa's other side. Amy reached for Melissa's boot again, but Josh stopped her. "If her ankle really is broken, we need to leave the boot on," he told her. "It can support the ankle better than anything else." He looked at Melissa. "Try stretching your ankle out," he said. "Just a little."

Melissa began to bend her ankle, but she winced and stopped. "It hurts," she whimpered.

"What exactly hurts?" Josh asked. "Just your ankle?"

Melissa nodded. "I can't feel the rest of my foot at all."

Josh's face tightened. "What do you mean, you can't feel it?"

"My toes are numb," Melissa said.

Josh was silent a moment, his face intent. "Sounds like the boot's cutting off circulation," he said at last. "In which case Amy's right, and it needs to come off after all. It must be too tight with all that swelling." He reached out and tugged at the boot, very gently.

Melissa screamed again.

Josh stopped pulling. He took a deep breath. "I guess we'll have to cut the boot off," he said.

"What?" Melissa looked at him as if he were out of his mind. "But they're almost new," she complained. "I've hardly worn them at all."

"I told you they were too tight for riding," Callie said. Melissa glared at her.

"If that boot's cutting off the flow of blood to your foot, you're going to be in worse shape the longer we wait," Josh said. He pulled a pocketknife out of his jeans. "Boots can be replaced. Your foot can't. All right?"

Melissa just nodded. Her face looked even paler than before, and Callie realized that her sister's ankle must hurt pretty badly. Still, Melissa wasn't helping things any.

Josh began cutting the suede boot. Melissa whimpered as he did; Callie couldn't tell whether that was from pain or because she didn't want to see her boot torn up. "I've never been so embarrassed in my life," Melissa muttered.

Amy stood, stretching stiffly. Her riding helmet was scuffed, and she rubbed the side of one leg. "I think we're all going to be pretty sore for a while," she said.

When Josh was done cutting, he carefully pulled the boot away. Melissa winced. Josh cut part of the leg of her jeans, too, rolling it halfway to her knee. He pulled her sock off.

Beneath the sock, Melissa's ankle was swollen to the size of a tennis ball and already turning purple.

Josh whistled. "You must have twisted that ankle pretty hard when you fell," he said. He gingerly touched it. Melissa whimpered.

"Try straightening your ankle out again," Josh said.

Slowly, wincing all the while, Melissa straightened her ankle most of the way.

Josh rubbed his chin. "I don't think it's broken," he said, "though it's hard to be sure beneath all that swelling. I'd feel better if a doctor looked at it. We need to find the horses."

Melissa tensed. "I'm not getting back on a horse."

"You don't have much choice," Callie said.

"I don't want to fall again. I won't ride. You can't make me." Melissa's voice sounded strangely young and petulant.

"Let's worry about that after we find the horses, okay?" Josh said.

"Right," Callie said. They already knew the horses were scared. For all they knew, the animals might be hurt, too. "Let's start looking already," Callie said.

An hour later there was still no sign of any of the horses. More than once they found hoofprints on the trail, only to lose the tracks in the underbrush. Amy did find a pair of saddlebags that had come loose, with some water, food, and other stuff inside. Callie found a second canteen with the cap loose; most of the water had leaked out.

By the time they returned, the sun was high in the sky, though the day was merely warm, not burning hot the way it would have been at the base of the mountains.

Melissa was sitting up, leaning against a tree. Since she couldn't wear her boot, Josh had bound her ankle with strips of Amy's jacket. The first-aid kit had been on Josh's horse, so they didn't have any other bandages. Amy hadn't complained when Josh said he needed to use the jacket. In fact, she'd torn it up herself.

Melissa's ankle was elevated on a large rock; Josh said that was generally a good idea with injuries.

Melissa had removed her riding helmet; her red curls were sweaty and plastered to her head. "Any luck?" she asked.

Josh shook his head. Melissa looked relieved. Didn't she even care whether the horses were okay?

"I think we're going to have to try to walk out," Josh said. "We'll take it slow. If Melissa leans on me, she shouldn't have to put any weight on her ankle."

"We can't leave the horses!" Callie said.

"The horses are the ones who got us here," Amy agreed. "We can't abandon them."

"It's not like we have a choice," Josh snapped. Then he lowered his voice. "Listen, I don't like abandoning any animal. Especially not Rusty—he's the first horse I've ever owned. Not to mention that I'm probably out of a job if those horses don't come home." Josh hesitated and took a deep breath. "But I really do want a doctor to look at that ankle. And the horses know this trail pretty well; with any luck they'll find their own way home."

Amy bit her lip but nodded in agreement. Callie didn't say anything. It wasn't as though Melissa's life was in danger or anything. She wanted to keep looking.

"We'll send someone to search for the horses as soon as we can," Josh said. "In the meantime—" He looked at Melissa. "Can you stand?"

Melissa nodded. Josh reached out his hand. Melissa took it and slowly pulled herself up, carefully keeping her weight on her right foot. She leaned on Josh, breathing hard.

"Now," Josh said, "put your arm around my shoulders and try hopping forward. Be careful not to lean on your foot at all."

Melissa did as he said. Her arms and shoulders were red with sunburn now—there hadn't been any sunscreen in the saddlebags they'd found—and she held them stiffly as she leaned on Josh. A few hours earlier, Callie thought, Melissa would have been glad to get close to Josh. Now she was trembling, as if even standing took some effort.

Melissa hopped one step forward, then another. Josh followed her. On the third step Melissa stumbled. Instinctively she put her left foot down to steady herself and stepped on it, hard. She screamed and pulled her foot up again, then began to sob loudly. Josh helped her sit back down on the ground.

"It hurts," Melissa cried over and over again. Callie had never seen Melissa cry that way before. She wished she could do something. She knelt by her sister's side and put a tentative arm around her shoulders, feeling awkward all the time.

Melissa pushed her roughly away. "Just leave me alone," she said.

"I was only trying to help," Callie told her.

"Like you could help with anything," Melissa said.

"You can't exactly walk out of here on your own." Callie turned fiercely away from her sister. Even when she tried to be nice, Melissa was still so mean.

Josh sighed. "I should have known you couldn't walk all the way back to the stables with that ankle, even leaning on someone. I guess I just didn't want to admit it. If we had even one horse, you could ride out." He took off his hat—he'd found it while they were looking for the horses—and ran his hand through his hair until it stood on end. "I think I'd better go out for help," he said at last.

"I'll come with you," Amy said at once.

Josh shook his head. "I'll make better time alone. Besides, you need to stay here and look after Melissa."

"I can do that," Callie said, though she doubted Melissa would let her do anything.

"You both can," Josh said.

"You're leaving us here?" Melissa's voice was suddenly panicked. "Alone?"

"I wish I had a choice," Josh said.

"Do you want me to try to walk again?" Melissa started to stand, but Josh stopped her.

"Wanting has nothing to do with it," he said. "I don't think you can. Not for six miles or more on uneven trails. Not if we had that much trouble managing just a few steps."

Amy rummaged through the saddlebags and pulled out the full canteen of water. "Here," she said. Her voice was tense, and she looked suddenly worried. "You'll need this," she told Josh.

Josh pushed the canteen back at her. "So will you," he said.

"We're not walking anywhere," Amy insisted. "And it's hotter down there. Take it."

"No," Josh said.

Amy thrust the canteen at Josh; Josh shoved it back. For a moment they stared at each other, neither of them willing to back down. They were both very serious, but Callie had to stifle a laugh. For the first time she could remember, Josh and Amy were almost fighting like brother and sister.

"Wait a minute," Callie said. She picked up the empty canteen she'd found. "Here. You can split it."

"So we can," Josh said. He opened the full canteen and started pouring the water into the empty one. He poured slowly and carefully, as if the water were a rare and precious substance.

In the desert—or even the forests above the desert—maybe it was.

"That's enough," Amy said.

"There are three of you," Josh told her. He poured some more water before stopping.

"You're hopeless," Amy said.

Josh grinned, and the tension in his face dissolved a little. "So are you." He slung the canteen over his shoulder and glanced at his watch. "It's nearly noon now," he said. "It took us five hours to get this far on horseback. I think I can do better than that on foot, since I'll be going downhill and not stopping to rest. If all goes well, Search and Rescue should reach you not too long after dark."

Callie shivered. The thought of calling a rescue team made everything seem much more serious. And the thought of being in the mountains after sundown scared her, too.

Josh glanced at the sky. The white clouds were now tinged with faint gray underneath. He looked at Amy. "There's an overhang about half a mile farther in," he said. "Not far from Marshall Springs Campground."

"I know," Amy said. "I used to play hide-and-seek there on camping trips, remember? Scared the heck out of you and Dad one time—"

"Well, it's there if you need shelter and can get to it," Josh interrupted. "After you've rested awhile, Melissa might feel more up to trying to walk again, at least a short way. I'll tell Search and Rescue to check the overhang if they don't find you here." Josh shoved his hands deep into his pockets. "Maybe the horses will show up after I leave. Maybe you should try looking for them some more. If you find them, start on home—you'll probably run into the searchers on the way."

"Quit worrying," Amy said, though she still sounded a little worried herself. "The first clouds of summer never do more than tease us. And we'll just huddle together for warmth if we need to. You know I can take care of myself—and of Callie and Melissa—well enough."

Josh shrugged, as if embarrassed. "So I worry about my kid sister sometimes."

Amy looked a little bit uncomfortable, too. "You need to get going," she said. "The sun isn't getting any higher while you wait."

Josh took a deep breath. "You guys be careful, okay?"

"Of course." Amy pushed him toward the trail. Josh started walking, then stopped and looked back. Amy gestured at him with her arms, shooing him along. Josh laughed and started walking again, much faster this time. Callie and Amy watched until he disappeared around a bend in the trail.

They were alone in the mountains. Somehow the fact hadn't hit Callie until Josh was out of sight. Her stomach felt like lead. If anything happened, there was no one to help them.

The trees near the trail rustled. For just a moment, Callie heard footsteps again, the way she had by the wall of the old homestead. A cold chill ran down her spine. She had the distinct feeling someone was watching her.

Callie looked around. She, Amy, and Melissa were the only people in sight. Maybe the rustling had just been the wind. Maybe she was imagining things yet again.

She hadn't imagined Star, though. How could she know that the other things she thought she heard weren't real, too?

"I hope Josh has enough water," Amy said. She was still staring down the trail. "It'll be so hot down there, and hiking alone is never really a good idea. . . ." Her voice trailed off.

Callie realized that Amy was more concerned about Josh than about being stranded. Josh was an adult; it hadn't occurred to Callie to think he'd have any problems. "I'm sure he'll be fine," Callie said.

"You're probably right," Amy told her. "It's just that sometimes I worry about my big brother, too."

Chapter Six

After a while Callie and Amy returned to Melissa and sat down beside her. "How are you feeling?" Callie asked.

"I'm sitting in the dirt with an ankle the size of a grapefruit," Melissa snapped. "How do you think I feel?"

Amy reached for the saddlebags and dumped their contents out on the ground in front of her. There were two peanut butter sandwiches, a bruised apple, some carrots, a thin paperback about the rise and fall of the Roman Empire (Amy really did read everything), a bag of trail mix, and a battered jacket that must have belonged to Josh.

Callie took off her helmet. Somehow she hadn't gotten around to doing that after she fell. Amy did the same. Amy's shoulder-length hair was tied back; she shook it loose.

"I'm thirsty," Melissa complained.

Callie picked up the canteen and handed it to her sister. "Here," she said.

Melissa took a sip. She sputtered. "The water's warm!" She threw the canteen away from her. As it hit the ground, water started dribbling out.

Callie jumped to her feet and ran after the canteen. She grabbed it and screwed the cap tightly shut. She shook the canteen. More than half of the water Josh had left them was gone.

She stormed back over to Melissa. "What did you do that for?" she demanded.

"It tasted awful," Melissa said.

"But this is all the water we have," Callie told her.

"So?" Melissa said. "Josh will be back soon enough."

"It'll take him four or five hours, at least— just to get back to the stables!" Callie's voice rose. "Whoever he calls needs five more hours to come in after us, too! Why are you being so stupid?"

"Callie—" Amy laid a calming hand on her shoulder. Callie hadn't even seen her friend come up behind her. "It's all right. It's not that hot up here. We'll make the water last."

Callie whirled away from Amy's touch. "I hate her!" Callie yelled. "I really hate her!"

"I don't exactly like you, either," Melissa muttered.

"Melissa doesn't feel well," Amy said. "You can't blame her for that."

"But she's always like this!" Callie said.

"You wouldn't understand—you and Josh always get along."

Amy laughed. "What makes you think Josh and I don't fight?"

Callie ignored her. After gritting her teeth and putting up with Melissa all the way into the mountains, she suddenly needed to get away. She turned and ran from the clearing, across the trail and into the trees on the other side. Amy called after her, but Callie ignored that too.

She ran, pine needles flying up beneath her feet. An animal that might have been a chipmunk scurried out of her path, but she barely noticed. She almost tripped over a thick root, but she kept going. Running felt good; she couldn't think about anything else while she ran.

A tingle ran down Callie's spine. She felt a familiar presence in a corner of her mind.

"Star?" Callie stopped short, skidding on the pine needles. She looked around, but Star was nowhere in sight. She still felt the horse's presence, though. Star didn't seem angry now, just hesitant and a little bit curious.

"Star, where are you?" Callie walked slowly forward, looking around her all the while. She nearly bumped into a huge boulder right in her path.

Behind the boulder, she heard a snort. Callie

caught her breath. Was Star standing on the other side of the rock? Very slowly, Callie walked around it.

Star wasn't there. Pepper was. The chestnut roan mare stood with her back to Callie, calmly munching on a bush.

Callie sighed. She liked Pepper, and she was relieved that the horse was okay, but she'd been so sure Star was there.

Pepper's ears perked up. She turned, looked at Callie, then walked cheerfully up to her and nudged her pockets. Callie laughed. She reached up and scratched Pepper behind the ears.

Out of nowhere Callie felt something—a surge of anger so fierce that she stumbled. She heard hooves crashing through the underbrush behind her. The running abruptly stopped. Callie turned around.

Star stood just a few yards away. Her coat shimmered silver. Her eyes were dark and incredibly deep.

Callie still felt Star's anger. Why was Star acting like this? She started toward the ghost horse. Star's ears went flat against her head. Her tail twitched. Callie stopped short. She closed her eyes, fighting tears, then opened them again.

"What's wrong with you?" she whispered. "It's me, Callie. Don't you know that?"

Star threw her head back and nickered. Behind Callie, Pepper nickered back. Star nickered again, more loudly. Then she lowered her head and ran. She raced past Callie, straight toward Pepper. Pepper backed wildly away.

"Stop it!" Callie yelled. "Leave her alone!" *Star*, she thought. *Stop it right now.*

Star stopped just a few feet from Pepper. Her ears were pinned back. She stared at the other horse, as close to glaring as a horse could manage. Pepper stared back, her tail twitching nervously from side to side.

Callie started toward the two horses. Pepper shied away, as if she feared Callie as much as Star. Callie felt bad for her. She'd already been scared once, after all. She walked up to Pepper and put a comforting hand on the horse's mane.

As she did, she felt Star's anger again, stronger than before. Star snorted fiercely. Startled, Callie stepped away from Pepper.

Star's anger subsided. Callie walked toward Pepper once more. Star's anger flared up again.

Callie whirled around to face Star. "You're jealous of Pepper!" she shouted, suddenly understanding.

Star stamped one hoof against the ground. "But how can you be jealous?" Callie said, staring at the horse. "Don't you know how much I've missed you? Riding Pepper doesn't change that." If anything, riding other horses reminded her of just how special Star was.

Callie stepped toward Star. Star snorted and backed away. Callie swallowed, fighting tears. *I love you*, she thought. *Don't you know that?*

Star stopped short. She lifted her head, then dropped it again, as if uncertain.

Can't I care about you and Pepper both? Callie asked. She hesitated, searching for a way to explain. *Just like you love me and Michael*, she thought. Star didn't move. Did the words even make sense to the horse? Callie tried picturing what she wanted to say. She thought about the night Star and Michael had left her. She pictured Star and Michael standing together in the mountains beneath a star-filled sky, Michael holding the horse. She pictured herself watching them, suddenly afraid Star didn't care about her anymore. She pictured Star turning away from Michael to look at her one last time, to remind Callie of her love.

The angry presence in Callie's mind subsided. For a moment Callie felt Star's hesitation. The horse took one step toward her, then another. Callie ran to her. Star nudged Callie's chest with her wet nose. Callie felt Star's love stretched like a rope between them, solid and sure once more.

Callie threw her arms around Star's neck and hugged her. She felt Star's soft coat against her cheek. She breathed Star's comfortable, horsy smell, like sweet summer grass. She ran her fingers through Star's mane over and over again.

She didn't know why Star had returned. She didn't know how long the horse would stay. All that mattered right then was that Star was with her once more.

She heard hooves pounding the dirt behind her. Still holding Star's mane, Callie turned around.

Pepper ran away from them, deeper into the forest. For a moment Callie stood frozen in place, unable to do anything but watch the horse disappear among the trees.

Then she heard something else: Amy running toward her, shouting, "Don't just stand there! Get on Star and ride after her!"

Chapter Seven

Callie grabbed Star's mane and jumped into the saddle. Amy gasped. Callie could guess why. Star was invisible to other people—and when Callie mounted her, she was invisible, too.

But if Star was invisible, how had Amy known the horse was there in the first place?

Callie didn't have time to worry about that. She gripped Star's reins. Amy was right; her only hope of catching Pepper was on horseback. *Chase her*, Callie thought.

Star burst into a fiery four-beat run. The gallop took Callie's breath away. She felt as though she and Star were flying. She'd missed riding like this so much.

She didn't need to tell Star which way to go, not with her legs and not with the reins. Star knew Callie's thoughts. She turned the right way without being asked. They were like one creature, thinking and moving together. Together they galloped in the direction Pepper had gone. Callie scanned the trees for some sign of the other horse. She and Star wound through the trees and over a thick blanket of pine needles. The wind was cool against the back of Callie's neck; the sweet smell of pine was everywhere.

Callie forgot they were stranded in the mountains. She forgot they were desperately chasing a runaway horse. She even forgot that she'd fled into the forest to get away from Melissa. All that mattered was that she was riding Star again. Callie laughed with joy. She felt laughter bubbling in Star, too.

The trees grew thicker as they ran. Star slowed to a canter, then a trot, then a walk. The underbrush thickened; rocks became more and more frequent. Callie ducked to avoid a branch overhead. Star slowed further.

Stop, Callie finally thought. Star came to a crisp, clean halt. Callie had never managed anything like that in her lessons, no matter how hard she'd tried.

She looked out into the forest. She saw endless stands of pine trees. A squirrel scampered up a tree, disappearing among its branches. A bird dipped just inches in front of Callie, then darted off into the forest.

Callie listened. She heard the wind rustling through the pines, the buzz of some insect, the sound of Star's breathing. Did she hear someone else breathing, too? The sound was gone before she could tell.

There was no sign of Pepper. Callie looked at the ground beneath her. There were no hoofprints—not from Pepper, and not from Star either, since as far as Callie could tell, the ghost horse never left any prints.

Callie sighed. She'd been sure Pepper had run this way, but she must have been wrong. She had no idea where to continue looking. She hoped Pepper was okay.

Star turned around before Callie asked her to. Together, they walked back toward the trail. Even at a walk, Star was graceful, her gait silky and smooth. Callie leaned down and hugged her.

"I love you," Callie whispered into her ear. "Don't you ever forget that again."

Amy waited where Callie had left her. She sat cross-legged on the ground, squinting into the forest. Even when Callie rode right up to Amy, her friend didn't see her. As soon as Callie dismounted, though, Amy gasped and jumped to her feet.

She stared at Callie, shaking her head, as if unable to believe Callie had just appeared out of thin air in front of her. "Wow," Amy said. "You really do disappear when you ride Star. I know you told me about that, but seeing it for myself is—well, it's amazing, that's what it is."

Callie just nodded. "I lost Pepper," she said.

She expected Amy to be disappointed, but Amy barely heard her. She stared past Callie, squinting again.

"Is Star still with you?" Amy asked. Her voice was low, almost reverent.

"Yeah," Callie said. As if in response, Star leaned her head on Callie's shoulder. Her nose was wet. "That tickles," Callie said, twisting away. Amy laughed.

Star seemed so solid and real to Callie. It was hard to believe sometimes that other people couldn't see her, that she really was a ghost.

"How did you know Star was with me before?" Callie asked.

"I knew because of what happened when you hugged her," Amy said. Her eyes went wide. "For just a moment you turned all shimmery. I could see the forest right through you. Then Pepper ran, and you turned around, and the picture snapped. You were real again. I figured you must've been holding Star. Nothing else made any sense. And when you mounted her and disappeared, I knew I was right."

Callie shivered. The idea of being transparent felt weirder than being invisible. It meant she'd been a little bit like a ghost herself.

Amy swallowed. "Do you think—" she began, then hesitated. "Do you think maybe I could touch Star?"

"You could try," Callie said. She didn't know

whether someone who couldn't see Star could still touch her. Callie moved to Star's side and draped an arm over her shoulders. "Can you still see me?" Callie asked. She wondered how close she had to be to Star before she turned transparent.

"Pretty much," Amy said. "Though you do seem a little fuzzy around the edges."

"My arm is right in front of Star's saddle," Callie explained.

Amy walked up to them. She stretched a trembling hand toward Star's neck.

The place where Amy touched Star shimmered. Amy's hand passed right through the horse. When Amy pulled her hand away, the spot turned solid once more.

"She's right there," Amy whispered. "I just can't touch her." Amy bit her lip; she seemed about to cry. Amy had wanted to meet and ride Star ever since she first heard about the ghost horse, but Callie hadn't known she'd wanted it that badly.

I wish Amy could see you, Callie thought to Star. She pictured the horse materializing in front of Amy. She pictured Amy's excited expression as she saw Star.

Amy gasped. She stretched out her hand again, and this time her palm rested against Star's neck. After just a moment her hand passed through Star once more. Amy smiled as she drew her hand away.

"I saw her," Amy said. Her eyes were suddenly bright. "Only for a few seconds, and she shimmered the whole time. But I touched her. She has the silkiest coat I've ever felt. Callie, she's gorgeous."

Had Star really made herself visible on purpose, just because Callie had asked her to? Callie hadn't known Star could control who saw her like that.

"Do you think I could ride her sometime?" Amy asked.

"I don't know," Callie said. "I guess that's up to Star." Star snorted, as if to say she'd think about it.

A gust of wind burst through the forest. It roared through the trees, and it blew Amy's hair into her face. Star stamped nervously at the ground.

The wind died as quickly as it had come. The air was suddenly much cooler. Callie smelled a strange, wet scent, like damp dirt, only heavier. The smell of pine needles was stronger than before, too.

Amy looked up; Callie followed her gaze. The sky was filled with gray clouds now, though patches of startlingly clear blue sky still shone between them. Callie wondered how the clouds had moved in so fast. Josh had only left about an hour before.

"I guess we're finally getting rain," Callie said. She'd never minded light rain. She liked how it felt against her skin. Given how dry Tucson was, she couldn't picture anything but light rain there.

Amy's face went pale. "What we're getting are monsoons."

Callie shuddered. "What are monsoons?" she asked, not sure she wanted to know. Amy had used the term once before, but back then Callie had assumed she was joking. Monsoons sounded like something that belonged on some far-off stormy island, not anywhere Callie lived.

"Summer thunderstorms," Amy said. "The clouds have been hanging around all week, but I didn't think they'd break today. Neither did Josh. And if we hadn't lost the horses, it wouldn't have mattered. Rain always hits the higher elevations first. If we started back on horseback now, we'd probably be well out of the way before any rain fell."

"But there were only a few clouds when Josh left," Callie said. Back in New York, storms never came in that fast.

The wind gusted again. The tree branches tossed wildly back and forth. In the distance, thunder rumbled.

Amy took a deep breath. "We'd better get

back to Melissa," she said. She started walking. Callie followed her.

Star followed Callie. Callie smiled. She patted Star. It felt so good to have her back.

Behind Callie and Star, a twig snapped. Callie whirled around. Someone—was it a man?—fled into the woods, disappearing among the tall trees. Callie caught a glimpse of dark hair. She called out after him.

Amy turned around. She followed Callie's gaze. "No one's there," she said.

"But someone was," Callie said. "He ran when I saw him." Callie hadn't imagined anything, not back by the stream and not on the trail while watching Josh leave. They were being followed.

Amy brushed her hair out of her face. She looked worried, but she only said, "There's nothing we can do about it now. We have to get back to Melissa."

"But what if he comes back?" Callie asked.

Amy's face tightened. She drew her arms tightly around herself. "I don't know," she said. "I guess we'd better just hope he doesn't." She turned and continued walking.

Callie stared into the woods a moment more. Why would someone follow them for so many miles? What did he want? Whatever he wanted, it couldn't be anything good; otherwise he wouldn't have run. Callie reached out for the comfort of Star's mane. Together they followed Amy back to the trail.

Melissa still sat in the clearing on the other side of the trail, huddled with her knees drawn to her chin. As Callie and Amy approached, she looked up. For a moment she seemed relieved. Then she scowled. "Nice of you to just run off and forget about me," she said. "I was beginning to wonder if you were ever coming back."

Callie was so tired of Melissa. And knowing they were being followed made her even more nervous and edgy. "I should have just left you here," she said.

"Don't say that!" Melissa's eyes grew large, and Callie realized she really had been afraid Callie and Amy would abandon her.

"Both of you stop it." Amy stepped between Callie and Melissa, as if ready to physically stop them from snapping at each other. Callie looked at her friend; Melissa just stared at the ground.

Amy took a deep breath. "Listen to me. It's going to storm soon, and I don't want to be outside when it does. We need to get to shelter, and we need to get there fast."

"It's going to rain?" Melissa looked up, as if seeing the clouds for the first time. Hadn't she heard the thunder a few minutes ago? "Why did

Josh let us ride here in the first place if it was going to rain?" Melissa went on. "And why'd he leave us here? Didn't he know any better?"

Amy clenched her fists. When she spoke again, though, her voice was calm. "Storms move in quickly here," she said. "We didn't know when we left that it was going to rain. Anyway, there's a sheltered overhang right near Marshall Springs Campground." She looked at Melissa. "How's your ankle?"

"It hurts," Melissa snapped. "What did you expect?"

"Can you walk on it at all?" Amy asked. Melissa just glared at her. Amy looked wistfully into the forest. "If only we still had Pepper," she said.

Callie followed her gaze. She hoped whoever was out there wouldn't find Pepper.

"I'm not getting on a horse," Melissa said.

"Since we don't even have a horse, that's not a problem," Amy told her.

Star walked up beside Callie and nudged her with her nose. Callie ran a hand along her mane. They did have a horse, only no one else could ride her.

Or could they? Star had turned solid for Amy, just for a moment. Could she stay solid longer for Melissa?

Callie pushed the thought fiercely aside. Even if Star could turn solid like that, Melissa was the last person Callie wanted riding her. No one but Amy even knew about Star. Callie didn't want to share her secret with Melissa.

"Maybe you could lean on both of us," Callie said.

"It's worth a try," Amy said. She reached out an arm. Melissa took it and stood. Melissa draped one arm around Amy and one around Callie. Together they started toward the trail. Star followed.

For the first few steps they did okay. Melissa could hop farther and faster when leaning on two people than when she'd leaned only on Josh. But Callie's shoulder was still sore, and Melissa's arm felt heavy and awkward. Callie kept stumbling over rocks and tree roots, too. Then, just as they reached the trail, Melissa's good foot slipped on a rock. Melissa flew forward, Callie and Amy with her. Amy regained her footing, but Callie tumbled to the ground. Melissa yelped as she landed on top of Callie.

"Ouch!" Callie wriggled out from under her sister and stood. Star trotted to her side. Callie felt the horse's concern. She scratched Star behind the ears, assuring her she was okay.

Melissa curled up into a ball and lay on the ground, sobbing. She looked awfully young just lying there like that. Callie felt suddenly bad for her. Had she hurt herself more when she'd fallen just now?

"I don't think this is going to work," Amy said. Melissa just kept crying. Thunder rumbled again, louder than before. Star pawed the ground uneasily. The light suddenly dimmed. Callie looked up. Clouds completely covered the sun. They were darker than before, more black than gray. Over a distant mountain peak, a bolt of lightning struck the ground.

Callie shivered. Michael and Star had died in a fire caused by lightning in the mountains. Callie had relived that fire with them, and she'd thought she was going to die in it. But the flames had only been ghost flames, and she hadn't been hurt at all. This storm was real, though. Anything that happened to them now would be real, too.

"We could try to carry her," Amy said, but she sounded doubtful. The wind picked up again, blowing the trees wildly about. This time it didn't die down. Callie drew her arms around herself.

She looked at Star. "Could Melissa ride you?" she asked out loud. Star just snorted.

Callie looked at her sister. Melissa was sitting up now, head between her knees, still crying. Melissa had always acted as if she was the one who was in charge and knew everything, yet she seemed so helpless now.

Callie thought about how Melissa always said mean things to her, about how she insisted

Callie was just a kid. She thought about how Melissa teased her, whispering things so low their parents couldn't hear. Callie thought of all the times their parents got angry at her and didn't notice what Melissa said at all. More than anything, Callie knew she didn't want Melissa to ride Star.

Callie thought instead about how Melissa had known, when they'd first moved to Tucson, that Callie was spending so much time outside at night. Melissa had never told their parents about that. Callie had never understood why.

She thought about how worried Melissa had seemed when Callie had returned from spending the entire night with Star and Michael in the mountains. At the time, Melissa's concern had surprised her. She hadn't expected Melissa to care about her that much. Now Callie almost understood. She didn't like Melissa, but she didn't want to see her hurt, either. Just thinking about it tied her stomach into knots.

"We could try to make a stretcher," Amy said doubtfully. "Though I'm not quite sure how we'd tie the wood together."

Callie took a deep breath. "No," she said. "I have a better idea."

Chapter Eight

Callie took Star's head in her hands. She stared into Star's deep eyes. The wind blew Star's mane around, giving her an almost wild look. The wind felt cold against Callie's bare arms. "I want Melissa to see you," she said.

Melissa looked up at the sound of her name. Her eyes were still red, but she'd finally stopped crying. "Who are you talking to?" she demanded. "What's going on?"

Callie didn't answer. *I want Melissa to see you*, she thought. *The way Amy saw you before, but for longer.* She pictured Star flickering into view in front of Melissa. She pictured Melissa riding the horse to shelter.

For a moment Star just stood there, staring back at Callie. Maybe this wasn't going to work after all. Maybe Amy had just been lucky. Maybe Star couldn't really control who saw her and who didn't.

Amy gasped. "Star's here," she whispered.

Melissa yelped. "Where did that horse come from?" Her voice was wild with panic.

Callie wasn't about to tell Melissa where Star came from. Needing to let her sister see the horse was bad enough. "This is Star," she said.

"It wasn't here a second ago," Melissa insisted. "It just appeared out of nowhere. Horses aren't supposed to do that." Still sitting, Melissa inched away from Star. "That horse isn't even one of ours. What's going on, Callie?"

Something wet brushed Callie's hand. Was it a raindrop? She couldn't tell. "You can ride Star to the overhang," she told Melissa. "That's all that matters."

"What do you mean, that's all that matters?" Melissa looked frantically around. "Who does that horse belong to? Maybe its owners can help us. I'd rather be helped by a person than a horse. I don't trust horses, not after mine threw me like that."

"Just because a horse spooks once is no reason never to trust horses again," Amy said quietly. "Horses have bad days and get scared, just like us."

"What time is it?" Melissa demanded. Her voice was desperate. "Isn't Josh due back soon?"

Amy glanced at her watch. "It's just after two. Josh has a long way to go yet." She looked at the sky. "He should at least be far enough along to beat the storm, though. It won't rain down below for a while yet."

"Him?" Melissa screamed. "What about us? And what about that horse? How'd it get here?"

"We won't get caught in the rain if you ride Star," Callie said, deliberately ignoring the second part of Melissa's question. The sky was very dark now, the clouds black and bruised. In the dim light, the green of the trees seemed much deeper than before, almost oppressive.

Was someone still watching them from within those trees? Callie shook the thought away. Amy was right; there was nothing they could do about that right then. They had to get to shelter.

"I won't do it," Melissa said. "I won't ride. Especially not if you won't even tell me where the horse came from."

A flash of blue lightning turned the world bright and stark. Thunder cracked through the air around them. Star's ears went back; she twitched nervously. Callie held her, thinking calming thoughts until she settled down.

In the distance, Callie heard a slow creaking sound, then a loud thud. The color drained from Melissa's face. "What was that?" she asked.

"A tree must be down," Amy said.

Melissa looked up at the swaying trees. She swallowed and turned back to Callie and Amy.

"Well, if you're going to make me ride, let's get it over with," she said.

Lightning flashed again. Thunder crackled, louder than before. Melissa stood. Callie led Star over to her, and Melissa stared nervously up at the horse. "How am I supposed to get up there?" she asked.

Amy laced her hands together and held them beside Star's left stirrup. "Rest your left knee in my hands," she said. "The same way you'd normally rest your foot in the stirrup. You can push yourself up from there."

Melissa hesitantly did as Amy suggested. She put her knee in Amy's hands, then grabbed the saddle. Star shifted uneasily.

Stop, Callie thought. Star stood stone still.

Melissa tried to pull herself up, but she couldn't pull high enough. She began to slide. Callie cupped her hands beneath her sister's right foot and pushed her up. Melissa fell into place in the saddle. She clutched the saddle horn and sat there, breathing hard. Her hands shook.

"Are you okay?" Callie asked.

"No, I feel dizzy. I want to get down. How far away is this place, anyway?"

"Half an hour or so," Amy said.

Melissa shifted uneasily in the saddle. "I want to get down," she said again.

Star snorted, as if picking up on Melissa's uneasiness. At the spots where Melissa touched Star and the saddle, the horse began to shimmer. The shimmering quickly spread to the rest of her body.

"No!" Callie screamed. *Stop,* she thought as hard as she could.

Star turned solid and real once more. Callie let out a breath. She hadn't realized that Star could disappear with someone on her back. Would Melissa crash to the ground if she did? Star was always solid for Callie, but Amy's hand had gone right through her at first. What would have happened to Melissa? Callie didn't want to think about it. *Don't do that again,* she thought. *Not while someone's riding.*

Star stamped one hoof; the gesture was like a shrug.

"What was that all about?" Melissa demanded. Apparently she—and Amy—hadn't noticed Star shimmering.

Callie swallowed. "Nothing," she said. Melissa gave Callie a long look, and even Amy glanced at her suspiciously. Callie didn't say anything more, though. There was no way to explain without telling Melissa more about Star, and Callie still wasn't willing to do that.

Amy ran back to the clearing and quickly repacked their saddlebags. She returned with both the bags and their riding helmets. Callie took Star's reins, preparing to lead her. She wasn't sure she needed to—Star would know which way Callie wanted to go—but she didn't want to explain that to Melissa either.

"Let's go," Amy said. She started along the trail. Callie followed, with Star walking beside her. Melissa yelped and clutched the saddle horn tighter. Callie wondered whether they should start toward home instead of heading for the overhang. Judging by the clouds and the lightning, though, the storm was too close now for them to beat the rain.

They followed the trail uphill. Callie watched Star nervously for a while, but the horse didn't shimmer again.

Beyond the trees to their right, Callie saw a rock wall. The wall got higher as they walked. The stream remained out of sight to their left, but the sound of its roaring grew louder. Had the rain already started somewhere out of sight, flooding the river as it fell?

Lightning flashed more and more often, blue-white bolts that branched off in every direction. Callie walked faster. She'd never seen lightning like that before.

The wind raised goose bumps on her arms. After the hot Tucson summer, she hadn't thought she'd ever be cold again. Thunder rumbled. She didn't hear any animals; they must have already fled the storm. The silence was eerie. Callie glanced into the forest. She didn't see anyone, but she couldn't shake the feeling they were still being watched. Callie swallowed. She'd heard too many stories about kids getting killed by strangers who followed them out to abandoned places.

Large, splattering raindrops began to fall. The rain quickly plastered Callie's clothes to her body. It dripped from Amy's long hair, and it soaked through Melissa's tank top. Melissa started shivering. Star snorted. Water fell all around her, but through the rain, the horse looked dry. Callie touched her silvery mane. It wasn't even damp. However solid Star might feel to Callie, the rain couldn't touch her. The fact made Star seem even more ghostly.

The trail veered right, toward the rock wall. They reached the wall, then turned left again, following the rock uphill. The wind grew wilder, blowing the tree branches crazily about. The rain fell harder, soaking everyone but Star. Finally Amy stopped short. Her wet hair hung limply around her shoulders. "This is it," she said.

At first Callie didn't see anything. Then she noticed that where they stood, the rock wall was actually several feet above the ground.

There was a crawl space beneath the rock, not much higher than Callie's waist, stretching back into darkness.

Callie and Amy helped Melissa out of the saddle. Callie was glad to see Melissa dismount. She still didn't like seeing her sister ride Star.

Melissa shivered harder than before. She leaned heavily on Callie as they stumbled to the overhang. They knelt down and crawled in. The air inside was warmer, and the ground beneath them was soft dirt. There was room enough to continue kneeling but not to stand.

They led Melissa to the back of the overhang, just a few yards in, where the dirt sloped up to meet the rock. Melissa curled up on the ground. "I'm cold," she complained. "And dizzy."

Callie touched Melissa's bare arm. It felt cold and clammy, much more so than Callie's own wet skin.

Amy rummaged through the saddlebags and pulled out Josh's jacket. "Here," she said. "This should help keep you warm." Melissa took the jacket and huddled beneath it. Remembering what Josh had said about elevating injuries, Callie slid the saddlebags beneath Melissa's legs.

"I'm tired," Melissa said. The ride seemed to have worn her out completely. "I hate horses," she muttered. Then she closed her eyes and fell asleep.

"Do you think she's okay?" Callie whispered to keep from waking Melissa up. She didn't like the way Melissa was lying there still, shaking.

"She's probably just cold and tired," Amy said. She bit her lip. "But you never know." Her eyes took on an odd, far-off look. "You can't ever be sure anyone's going to be all right, not really." Callie wondered whether she was worrying about Josh again. Or maybe she was thinking about her parents. They'd died without warning, in a car crash. How could you count on anything after that?

Without speaking, Callie and Amy crawled to the front of the overhang. Star stretched her neck down and poked her nose in at them. Her mane, still dry, was blown about in all directions. Callie reached out and brushed it away from Star's dark eyes. Even in the dim light, Star glimmered.

Without warning, Star turned away and looked out into the rain. Her ears perked forward. Callie didn't feel any concern from Star, but she could tell the horse was curious. Had Star seen the person who was following them? Callie tensed. She scanned the trees, looking for any sign of another human being.

"Is someone out there?" Amy asked, stiffening.

"I don't know." Callie kept looking. Suddenly she did see something—a shadowy figure among the trees. She felt as though he was watching her intently, even though she couldn't see him very well. Callie nudged Amy and pointed, but all at once the shadow was gone.

"I don't see anything," Amy said.

"Neither do I," Callie told her. "Not anyone."

Amy drew her arms around her knees. "Why would someone follow us all day?" she asked. "If he wanted to hurt us, wouldn't he have done it by now? He had plenty of chances, especially when the three of us were separated before."

Callie didn't answer. She didn't know why, any more than Amy did.

Star lowered her head, still looking out into the rain. Callie felt as if the horse was guarding them. She was glad. She felt safer with Star there.

Callie heard a rush of water. Without warning the rain turned into a torrent. Rain raced off the edge of the overhang in wide streams. Wind whistled through the air and blew water onto Callie's bare arms. She and Amy crawled farther back again, nearly bumping into Melissa as they did. Beyond the water, Callie saw Star, continuing to guard them in spite of—or maybe because of—the heavy rain. By the way Amy stared outside, Callie knew that Star was still visible. Callie wondered why. Maybe Star wanted to make it clear she was guarding Amy and Melissa, too.

Without warning, Amy laughed.

"What's so funny?" Callie asked.

Amy grinned. "We got to see a waterfall," she said. "Not the one at Marshall Springs, and not the way we planned. But in a way this is more interesting."

"How?" Callie asked.

"Because we're seeing the waterfall from behind," Amy said. "How many people get to do that?"

Chapter Nine

The rain pounded the earth into mud. It turned the trail into a river. Lightning flashed again and again. Thunder echoed through the forest. The waterfall turned into a thick wall of water through which Callie could barely see the outside world.

After what seemed like hours, the torrent changed back to a normal downpour. The wall of water became a trickling waterfall once more. The wind died down. Through the waterfall Callie saw the branches of the trees, dripping more water. Water hung in the air, too, turning it to gray mist. If lightning struck now, Callie doubted there'd be anything dry enough to catch fire. Everything smelled wet and muddy. Callie inched back up to the edge of the overhang.

A stray gust of wind splattered her and Amy with water.

Callie sighed. She was tired of the rain, and she was tired of worrying about who might be following them. "Do you think it'll ever stop raining?" she asked.

"Oh, but I love rain," Amy told her. "Especially the first rain of summer. Of course, I love it more now that we've made it to shelter."

Callie took a deep breath, inhaling the earthy smell of mud and wet forest. It was so different from the dusty desert smell she'd grown used to. After the long, dry summer, the rain really was amazing. Even if they were stranded in it.

Another gust of wind drenched both girls. "We're never going to get dry," Callie said.

A grin crossed Amy's face. "So stop trying." She crawled outside, through the waterfall, and held her arms out to the rain. She twirled around in a circle as the rain soaked her through.

"You're crazy," Callie said.

For just a moment Amy's face turned serious. "You have to be a little bit crazy at a time like this. It's the only way to keep from losing it completely." She grinned again. She cupped both hands beneath the waterfall, filled them with water, and without warning threw the water at Callie.

Callie yelped. She scurried out of the overhang, filling her hands with some water to throw back at Amy. Soon they were laughing and screaming at the same time as they ran around in the rain, flinging water back and forth.

Star snorted and trotted over to them, nudging Callie with her nose as if to make sure she was all right.

We're fine, Callie told her, still laughing. Star snorted again and walked back to the mouth of the overhang. Callie knew that Star would stay for as long as she needed her there.

Finally she and Amy crawled back beneath the overhang, still laughing.

"Of course, that was a really stupid thing to do," Amy said. "We're going to be colder than ever now that we're wet again."

"Yeah," Callie agreed. Her arms were covered with goose bumps. But she didn't regret getting soaked. She'd needed to do something silly. While she was laughing, she couldn't think too hard about being stranded, or about being followed, or about the disturbing way that Melissa kept tossing and moaning in her sleep. Callie and Amy had been taking turns checking on her. Her skin was still clammy, though not quite as bad as before. She'd stopped shivering, at least.

Amy stared through the waterfall. "Star really is beautiful," she said. Her voice turned strangely intense. "I wish I could ride her someday."

Callie leaned back, gazing up at the overhang's stone ceiling. "You've always been so interested in Star," she said. "Why?" As she spoke, she realized it was a silly thing to ask. Who wouldn't be curious about Star? Yet Callie couldn't shake the feeling that there'd always been something different about Amy's curiosity. She wasn't sure what.

Amy leaned back beside her. For a long time she was silent, and Callie thought maybe she'd decided not to answer the question. Amy ran a hand along the damp stone above her. "This is going to sound really stupid," she said.

"I won't laugh," Callie told her.

Amy sat up again. She scooped up a handful of damp pine needles and stared at them. "Star's a ghost," Amy said. "But you can still see her, and touch her, and even talk to her. I figure that if I can see Star . . . well, maybe one day I can see my mom and dad, too. Maybe Star can show me how." Amy threw the pine needles outside; the wind blew them away. "Like I said, it's pretty stupid."

Callie sat up beside her. "I don't think it's stupid," she said. "I wonder—" she began, then cut herself off.

"What?" Amy asked.

"Well, I was thinking about how you couldn't see Star before, even though she was standing right in front of you. I wonder whether your parents might sometimes be standing right by you, too, only you don't know about it."

Amy smiled. "I like that," she said. "I don't know whether I believe it, but I want to."

They stared into the rain—and at Star—in silence for a while. Were there really other ghosts around them that Callie just couldn't see? She thought of the homestead wall they'd seen earlier. Were the old owners still there, watching people walk through their house? What determined who became a ghost and who didn't?

A shadow among the trees on the far side of the trail caught Callie's eye. The shadow moved slowly toward them. Callie's breath caught in her throat. She strained for a better look, but the air was too misty to see much.

"Who's there?" Callie called. "What do you want?"

The shadow just stood there. For a moment he seemed to shimmer; then he was gone again. He must have disappeared into the mist.

Which meant he was still out there, watching them.

At dusk the rain still fell. Callie and Amy took the food out of the saddlebags. They woke Melissa and offered her some. Melissa took a few bites of the apple, then rolled over and went back to sleep.

Callie and Amy split the rest of the food. They hadn't eaten since their snack that morning. After a peanut butter sandwich, two carrots, and some trail mix, Callie was still hungry.

Amy held the canteen under the waterfall until it was full. She'd already done that once, but they'd drunk some since then. At least they didn't have to worry about not having enough water anymore. Amy took a long gulp, then handed the canteen to Callie. "Did you know you can live for weeks without food, as long as you have enough water?" Amy asked. "I read that somewhere."

Callie took a drink. "I think we have enough water to last a year," she said. That didn't stop her stomach from rumbling, though.

Dusk faded and darkness fell, without any of the colors that were usually part of Tucson sunsets. The gray clouds simply darkened into night. The clouds hid the moon; the night was darker than any Callie remembered. She waited for her eyes to adjust, but her hand was never more than a shadow in front of her face. Outside, Star was a larger shadow. Callie kept thinking about the other shadow she'd seen. Was he still watching them? What did he want?

"Amy?" Callie asked.

"Yeah?"

"Can rescue workers come in the rain?"

"Not if it's this heavy," Amy said. "The

washes will all be flooded. They'll leave as soon as it lets up, though. Which will probably be sooner down below than up here."

Callie thought about her dad and how he was always telling her no place was safe after dark. He must be worried sick. Given that someone was still out there, he might have reason to be worried.

"We're spending the night here, aren't we?" Callie said.

Amy nodded. "Sure looks that way, doesn't it?"

Something slunk up to the overhang. Not a person this time—an animal. It peered inside, as if curious what was there. Callie scuttled back; Amy did the same.

It was shaped like a dog, only leaner and sleeker, with a long, drooping tail. Even in the darkness its eyes shone like dark coals. A coyote. Callie froze. She didn't know how dangerous coyotes were, and she didn't want to find out.

Star nickered. The sound echoed above the pounding rain. The coyote turned abruptly and ran, disappearing into the night.

Callie let out a breath. "Do coyotes ever hurt people?" she asked.

"Not usually," Amy said. "They prefer to pick on things their own size. And we're at too low an altitude to have any trouble with bears." She bit her lip. "At least, I *think* we are."

Callie drew her arms around herself. She was very glad Star still stood outside.

"How tired are you?" Amy asked.

Callie yawned, even though she felt too tense to sleep. She wanted to stay awake until the rain stopped and the rescue workers came, but she had to admit she was tired. She felt as though she'd been awake forever, and not just since very early morning.

"How about we take turns keeping watch?" Amy said. "Between whoever you saw outside and the fact that we need to keep an eye on Melissa, someone has to stay up. I can go first, if you want."

Callie nodded. "Wake me up if you see anything," she said. Then she leaned back against the soft dirt. She didn't really expect to be able to sleep, but as soon as she closed her eyes, she began to drift off.

She heard the rain outside—pattering against the stone, brushing against the pine needles, soaking into the ground. She hadn't known rain had so many different sounds. Around her she smelled the sweet, heady scent of damp pine.

Even in the rain, even with her eyes closed, the landscape around Callie was beautiful. Tucson seemed to be like that, in the desert and the mountains both. You just couldn't forget the beauty all around you. Callie couldn't believe that when she'd first arrived, she'd found the mountains ugly and the desert lifeless.

Outside, an owl hooted. Something crashed through the trees and then was silent. Surrounded by the sounds of the forest and the comfortable feeling of Star's presence, Callie fell asleep.

Chapter Ten

When Callie woke, the world was quieter. She heard only the soft patter of water dripping through branches. The rain had finally stopped.

She sat up, shook herself awake, and crawled to Amy's side. Amy's eyes were open, but she kept blinking to stay awake. Outside, Star was taut and alert. Callie looked beyond the horse. The night was still very dark; Callie couldn't tell whether anyone else stood out there or not.

Callie nudged her friend. "My turn to keep watch," she said.

Amy nodded. She crawled back and curled up on the ground. Within moments Callie heard her snoring lightly.

Callie's legs were stiff from sitting inside so long. She felt uneasy at the thought of going outside, but she really couldn't bear to sit much more, either. How many hours had she spent beneath the overhang by now?

She stepped outside and stood, careful to stay close to the outcrop. She stretched out one leg, then the other. It felt good to stand again. Star walked up to her. Her silver-gray coat seemed to glow in the dark night. Callie ran her fingers through the horse's mane. She hugged her, inhaling the sweet smell of horse. "Thank you for staying here," Callie whispered.

Water dripped from the edge of the overhang and from the tall trees. The running water along the trail was only a trickle now. Callie took a deep breath. The air smelled incredibly clean, as if the rain had washed all the dust away.

Now that the rain had stopped, Callie wondered if Melissa could ride Star out of the mountains. She didn't know how they would explain Star, though, if they met the search-and-rescue team along the way.

Callie looked up. She saw clouds, much thinner than before, scuttling across the sky. Moonlight shone around their edges. All at once the clouds parted and the full moon broke through, casting silver light on everything. The water on the rocks shone; the droplets on the tree branches glittered like diamonds. Without warning, the whole world had turned to magic. Callie took another breath. The world was perfect, sparkling, frozen in place.

From beneath the overhang, Callie heard someone sobbing. It had to be Melissa.

Callie didn't want to go inside. But she hugged Star one more time, then turned away and crawled back beneath the overhang. Melissa was sitting up, hands wrapped around her knees, rocking back and forth as she cried. Callie crawled to Melissa's side. She touched Melissa's arm; her skin didn't feel at all cold or clammy now. Melissa flinched away from her.

"What's wrong?" Callie asked as gently as she could. "Are you still cold? Does your ankle hurt?"

"My ankle's just fine," Melissa snapped. "Everything's wonderful! Can't you tell?" In the faint moonlight, Melissa's eyes were sharp and angry.

"Just go away," Melissa said. "Go outside and play with your stupid old horse. That's all you really care about, anyway."

Callie sighed. It figured that as soon as Melissa felt just a little bit better, she'd be back to being obnoxious. "Why are you always so mean?" Callie asked. "Why do you make things so hard?"

Melissa wiped her nose on the side of her arm. "I'm not the one who makes things difficult, Callie. But you wouldn't understand. You never do. You're just a kid."

"Will you quit saying that?" Callie yelled. Her voice echoed off the stone. Amy rolled over in her sleep but didn't wake. Callie struggled to lower her voice. "I'm not that much younger than you are." After all that had happened that summer—moving, meeting Star, even being stranded in the mountains now—Callie felt even less young than she had when she'd first arrived in Arizona. In some ways Melissa didn't seem older than her at all anymore.

"You know," Callie snapped, "if it weren't for me, you'd still be lying out in the rain somewhere."

"If it weren't for you, I wouldn't have come on this stupid trail ride to begin with," Melissa said.

"No one made you come," Callie told her. "I don't know why you did. I wish you hadn't."

"You wouldn't understand," Melissa said again. "You actually like living here."

"You don't?" Callie had hated Tucson when she'd first arrived—Melissa had teased her about all the complaining she did—but she'd fallen in love with the desert and the mountains. "You told Mom and Dad you liked it here. You made fun of me every time I said I didn't."

"I hate this place!" Melissa screamed. Amy rolled over again. Callie saw her friend open her eyes, then quickly close them, as if she didn't want to interfere with the argument.

"I hate the desert," Melissa said. "I hate the heat. I hate the fact that we ever left New York. There's nothing for me to do here all day.

It's not like I have any friends here. Not like you." Melissa's voice caught. She swallowed. "There isn't anyone around my age where we live, and after I made such a fool of myself today, I'm sure Josh hates me."

"Everyone fell," Callie said. "You didn't make a fool of yourself by doing that."

"I don't even like horses." Melissa sniffled. "I only went riding because I was getting sick and tired of never having anything to do. Well, also because of Josh. He *is* awfully cute, you know."

Amy coughed loudly in her supposed sleep, but didn't say anything.

"There are all sorts of things to do during the day here," Callie said. "You can go walking, or read outside, or—"

"Maybe you like that sort of stuff, Callie, but I don't," Melissa said. "Besides, it's too hot to go outside here. And there are only reruns on TV in summer."

"Well, if you stay inside all the time, of course you're going to be unhappy," Callie said.

Melissa sighed. "I knew you wouldn't have any idea what I was talking about. I don't know why I'm even bothering to try to explain. Tucson's just an awful, dusty place, and there are all sorts of weird animals—I don't see how anyone could like it here."

"It's not dusty now," Callie said, glancing out at the dripping trees.

Melissa rolled her eyes. "You know what I mean." After a moment she added bitterly, "You're lucky you like horses. I bet you'd hate this place, too, if you didn't have your lessons to keep you busy."

Callie didn't answer. She and Melissa slipped into silence. Melissa closed her eyes but didn't sleep. Callie stared at her awhile. She didn't want to keep feeling bad for Melissa, but she couldn't help it.

Callie turned away from Melissa, crawled to the front of the overhang, and stared outside instead. The moon had slipped halfway behind a cloud and only dimly lit the ground below.

Was Melissa only obnoxious because she was so unhappy? Callie didn't believe that; even back in New York, she and Melissa had never gotten along. But Melissa had been even harder to deal with since they'd moved. Callie always yelled more and lost her patience faster when she was unhappy. Maybe Melissa was the same way.

A sudden sound among the trees drew Callie back to the present. She tensed, then peered out across the trail. She saw the shadowy figure watching her again. He crossed the trail and started toward her. Callie scuttled back deeper beneath the overhang.

The shadow stopped at Star's side. Fear trickled down Callie's spine. What if the stranger tried to hurt Star?

Star didn't seem nervous, though, and she didn't try to scare the stranger away. She stood very still as he laid one hand on her mane.

Callie squinted outside for a better look. She realized that the stranger wasn't a man after all, but a boy. A boy not much older than Callie, with dark hair, dark eyes, and a battered cowboy hat.

Callie blinked. She knew who he was. When she'd first moved to Tucson she'd dreamed about him almost as often as she'd dreamed about Star.

"Michael," Callie whispered. It was Star's real owner. Or rather, his ghost.

At first Callie was relieved. Michael seemed unlikely to run out and attack her, after all. But she still didn't know why he was there or why he'd followed her for so many miles. And he was still a ghost. Who knew what he wanted?

There was only one way to find out. Callie took a deep breath, crawled out from under the overhang, and started toward him.

Michael looked up at the sound of her footsteps. Faint silver light played over his features. At first Callie thought it was just moonlight.

But she realized that she could, just barely, see through Michael. He wasn't quite as solid as Star was.

Michael tensed as she approached. "Get away," he said. His voice was low and angry. Callie stopped short.

"It's me," Callie said. Then she remembered that the one time she'd seen Michael in person, he hadn't noticed her at all.

"I don't know who you are," Michael said. He tightened his grip on Star's mane. "All I know is that you keep taking Star away from me." He suddenly sounded more frightened than angry. "She's my horse. You'd better leave her alone."

Callie shook her head. What was Michael so worried about? "Do you think I'm going to hurt her?" she asked. "I'd never hurt Star. I love her as much as you do."

"No one loves Star as much as I do," Michael snapped. "Not my family, not anyone."

"That's not true," Callie said. She felt Star's love for them both, strong and real. Star could care about more than one human, just as Callie could care about more than one horse.

Michael opened his mouth, as if to say something. He took a step toward her. Callie felt a cold chill down her spine, nothing like Star's comfortable tingling. She backed away. Michael took another step. Then, without warning, he turned and fled into the woods. Callie wrapped her arms tightly around herself. She still felt cold, though the shivery chill had evaporated when Michael ran.

Star snorted and walked over to Callie, resting her head on Callie's shoulder. She wanted to be with Callie, no matter what Michael said. Callie hugged the horse tightly. Against Star's warmth, the cold feeling disappeared.

What did Michael mean when he said Callie kept taking Star away, anyway? Today was the first time she'd seen Star in weeks. In fact, the last time Callie had seen Star had been when she returned the horse to Michael. Callie felt suddenly bitter. Star had left *her*, after all, and somehow she'd coped with it.

But Michael and Star had died together. Maybe that made things different. It had to make things different, didn't it?

Star pawed the ground uneasily. Callie pushed all thoughts of the horse's death aside and hugged her even tighter. Behind her, beneath the overhang, she heard Melissa moving restlessly about.

Was Melissa right when she said Callie liked Tucson only because of the horses? Becoming friends with Amy had helped, too, but if Callie hadn't met Star, would she still hate living there? There was no way to know.

Melissa hadn't met anyone like Star, though, and she was still miserable.

113

Callie heard scuffling at the mouth of the overhang. Melissa crawled out and stood, leaning heavily on the stone wall. In the moonlight her eyes were puffy, her face drawn. "Who were you talking to?" she asked.

"No one," Callie said.

"I don't believe you," Melissa said. "I also don't believe that this horse appeared out of nowhere, or that nothing went on when you spent all those nights outside in the backyard." Melissa stared at her. "You're so weird sometimes, Callie. And ever since we moved, you've been up to something. What is it?"

"Nothing," Callie said.

"Is there some guy you're seeing?" she asked. "Is that who Michael is?"

Callie laughed out loud at that. "Why would I want to stay out all night with some boy?" Was that all Melissa ever thought about?

"Then what's going on?"

"Nothing," Callie said again. Melissa just kept staring at her. Callie knew her sister didn't believe her. "Why do you care, anyway?" Callie asked.

"Oh, don't be stupid." Melissa's expression turned strange. "Anyone with half a clue knows you've been up to something the past couple of months. Something unusual, maybe exciting. We all want exciting things to happen to us, Callie. You're not the only one."

Callie's eyes widened. Her sister was using different words than she would have, but she knew what Melissa was saying. She wanted to feel special and magical. Callie hadn't thought Melissa cared about that sort of thing.

She turned away from Melissa's sharp gaze. She focused on Star instead. Star was magical. Callie had known that from the very first time they'd met.

Star nudged Callie with her nose. Callie had a sudden image of the two of them riding together, racing through the forest. Star wanted to run with her again; Callie felt it. Callie wanted to ride, too.

The clouds had parted once more while Callie and Melissa spoke. The moon was bright enough to see by. Melissa was awake, and she seemed to feel much better now. Amy was awake, too, though she was pretending not to be. Surely there'd be no harm done if Callie left for a short ride. Michael might mind, but he'd run away, and it wasn't his decision, anyway.

Callie turned to face Star. For a moment she stared into the horse's dark eyes. Then she gathered up the reins and jumped into the saddle.

Melissa turned away and crawled back beneath the overhang. Callie thought she heard her sister crying yet again, but she wasn't sure.

Maybe it was just the wind blowing through the trees. Melissa hardly ever cried. She hardly ever whined or complained, either—those were things she teased Callie about doing. Yet ever since Melissa had fallen, she'd been different. It was weird. How was Callie supposed to tell which Melissa was real?

It didn't matter, Callie told herself fiercely. How Melissa felt wasn't her problem.

Yet she sat on Star's back for a long time, staring at the overhang. Everyone should have a chance to feel magic if they really wanted to, she thought. Even Melissa.

Callie jumped out of the saddle, back to the ground again. "Melissa," she finally called.

Melissa poked her head out. She looked tired. "What?"

"I'll share the magic with you," Callie said.

Melissa shook her head, looking at Callie as if she were crazy. "What magic? What are you talking about?"

"I want you to ride Star again," Callie said.

Chapter Eleven

Melissa crawled outside. From the expression on her face, Callie knew her sister still thought she was crazy.

"How's your ankle?" Callie asked.

"Better. It hurts, but not as much as before. And I'd like to avoid adding any other injuries to the list, so just get that horse out of here, okay?" Melissa scowled. "I don't want to ride it. I don't want to ride any horse again, ever. Don't you understand that?"

"But Star's different," Callie said.

"It's a horse," Melissa said.

Now that Callie had decided to let Melissa ride, she wanted her sister to see just how magical Star really was. She wanted Melissa to see how magical the trees and the mountains were, too.

And she wanted Melissa to ride before she changed her mind. She still wasn't very comfortable letting Melissa ride Star, even though she knew it was the right thing to do.

Callie bit her lip, wondering how to convince

her sister. "I'll tell you where Star came from," she blurted. As soon as she spoke, she regretted the words. She didn't want to share all her secrets with Melissa, after all.

Melissa's face turned thoughtful, though. "All right," she said. "Where?"

"I'll tell you afterward," Callie said quickly. If Melissa knew Star was a ghost now, she'd probably never ride. She'd be afraid to, even more than she was afraid to ride horses in the first place.

Melissa nodded. "All right," she said. "I'll do it."

From beneath the overhang, Callie heard Amy coughing again. Amy should be the one riding Star; she wanted to so badly. Maybe Amy could ride when Melissa was through.

Melissa hopped to Star's side. Her hands trembled; she was still scared. But when Callie cupped her hands beneath Star's stirrup, Melissa rested her knee there. As Melissa grabbed the saddle Callie felt Star's confusion. Star didn't understand why Melissa was riding again, rather than Callie.

Callie didn't know how to explain. Instead she pictured Melissa on the horse, assuring Star this was what she wanted. Star seemed to accept that; she didn't fidget as Melissa tried to pull herself up. When Melissa began to slide, Callie pushed her, and Melissa scrambled awkwardly into the saddle. She sat there, looking uncomfortable, hands clutching the saddle horn, glancing around.

Callie handed Melissa the reins. Melissa released her hold on the horn and took them, her hands still shaking. If Melissa was this nervous, would she even appreciate Star as she rode? Or worse, would Star pick up on her nervousness and try to shimmer away again? Callie didn't think so—Star had seemed to understand when Callie told her not to do that—but there was no way to be sure.

Melissa took a deep breath. "Let's get this over with," she said.

Walk, Callie thought. She pictured Melissa riding, Star solid and real beneath her. Star started forward. Melissa yelped. *Slow*, Callie thought. *Easy*. Star settled into the most gentle walk Callie had ever seen. Her hooves squished in the mud beneath her. She was leaving hoofprints—light ones, much fainter than most horses would leave, but real nonetheless. She'd never done that before.

Did her leaving prints have something to do with the fact that other people could see her? When she turned solid for other people, did she also become solid enough to leave marks in the mud? Yet the rain hadn't touched her, so she couldn't be completely solid, could she?

Star and Melissa followed the trail uphill,

Callie walking beside them. The rock wall still loomed to their right, but it grew shorter as they walked, until it was only about twice Callie's height, and then even shorter than that.

Slowly Melissa stopped shaking. "Star is nicer than most horses," she admitted. For several moments she didn't say anything more.

Star slipped in the mud. Melissa tensed. "Stop!" she yelled. "Whoa!" She pulled back on the reins.

Stop, Callie thought.

Star stopped and stood still, waiting.

"She listens," Melissa said. She sounded surprised.

"All horses listen," Callie said. "Most of the time, anyway. You just have to know how to ask." She thought about her own lessons with Pepper. She hoped the mare was okay. Maybe with more practice, she'd learn how to ask things so that Pepper would listen, too.

"Walk," Melissa said. Star started forward once more, this time without a thought from Callie. Melissa leaned forward and tentatively stroked Star's neck. After a moment she began to slide; she quickly sat back up.

Moonlight still reflected off the wet rocks. The edges of the clouds still shone. "Isn't it beautiful?" Callie said, pointing to the round, bright moon and the glistening rocks.

Melissa followed her gaze. "But they're just

clouds and rocks," she said. Her voice wasn't mean this time, but she really didn't understand. Maybe even Star couldn't make Melissa appreciate the magic of the mountains.

They rounded a bend in the trail. The rock wall suddenly disappeared; the trail leveled out. Callie pointed to the swaying branches and glistening trees all around them, but Melissa didn't seem to care. Callie commented on the rich smell of pine, but Melissa just shrugged.

Then without warning Melissa cried, "Whoa!" and pulled back on the reins.

"What is it?" Callie asked. "What's wrong?"

For the first time since she'd mounted Star, Melissa smiled. "Look at that," she said. She pointed to their right. Only a few yards beyond them, the mountain dropped sharply away. Far below, the lights of Tucson glittered on the desert floor. The city stretched for miles, stopping only when it hit another mountain range. Callie had been so busy watching the sky and trees that she hadn't noticed when the city came into view.

"Do you think that's the whole city or only part of it?" Melissa asked. "The lights are gorgeous from up here. It's much smaller than New York, but it's still pretty cool, don't you think?"

"I guess so," Callie said.

"You can see all the streets, even though it's so far away." Melissa's voice held the same awe Callie had felt the first time she rode into the mountains. "You can just imagine all the exciting things that are going on down there. You can imagine all the different people. It's so alive."

To Callie, the mountains and the animals in them were much more alive then any cold, distant lights. Still, she stood beside Melissa and Star, watching the city glow. She should have known Melissa wouldn't find magic in the same things she did. Maybe what was magical and special just depended on who you were.

"You promised me something," Melissa said. Her eyes never left the city, but her hand tightened around Star's reins. "Where did this horse come from?"

Callie reached up and scratched Star behind the ears. For a moment she hesitated. Then she took a deep breath and told Melissa Star's story, from the moment the horse had first appeared in the yard, to her dreams about Star and Michael, to the night Star left her.

Melissa gasped when Callie told her Star was a ghost. Still sitting on Star's back, Melissa reached a hand out to touch the horse, but she didn't interrupt the story.

When Callie was through, both girls were silent, watching the lights.

"Why didn't you tell Mom and Dad about Star?" Melissa asked at last. "That's what I would have done."

"Mom and Dad would never have let me keep riding," Callie said.

"So?" Melissa said. "I would have told them anyway."

Callie's cheeks turned hot. She fought not to get angry. "But I'm not you." To herself she thought, *I don't want to be.*

"I didn't say you were," Melissa said. "It's just that I would have been so scared, especially when those weird dreams started. I would have had to tell someone. But then, you've always been braver than I am. Ever since we were little. I used to think that was just because you were too young to know any better."

Was she really all that much braver than Melissa? Callie wasn't sure. One thing she did know, though. "I'm not a little kid," she said.

Melissa looked at her. "No," she said. "I guess you're not." She turned back to the city. "It's strange in a way," she continued. "How you can grow up in the same house as someone, yet be so different. Don't you think so?"

"Yeah," Callie said. She thought about Amy

and Josh. They were a lot alike; that was why they got along so well. But she and Melissa weren't Amy and Josh. Maybe that was okay.

Callie reached up and squeezed her sister's hand. Melissa looked surprised; then she squeezed back.

"I'm glad you're feeling better," Callie said. She felt she should say something more, but she wasn't sure what. She turned and started back toward the overhang. Melissa and Star followed.

Even as they walked, Callie knew that she and Melissa weren't going to stop fighting completely. But maybe they'd fight less. That would be worth something, wouldn't it? They wouldn't suddenly become best friends—but maybe they didn't need to be enemies, either.

Michael was standing by the overhang again when they returned. Callie felt the same cold chill she'd felt from him before. She wanted to turn and run away, but instead she bit her lip and kept walking. She wasn't going to leave Star just because Michael wanted her to.

Michael watched them approach. How much time had he spent watching her like that during the past day and night, somewhere out of sight? The thought was creepy; it made Callie feel even colder.

Melissa didn't seem to notice Michael, but Star did. Her ears perked up. Callie felt Star's enthusiasm as she walked the last few steps to him.

At the sight of Star, Michael smiled. Then he looked at Callie. His face had a strange expression, not as angry as before, but a lot more confused. Callie had the feeling he was trying to figure something out, but she didn't know what.

Michael patted Star on the shoulder. For a moment he stared at Star and Callie both, his face so intense that Callie could barely stand to look back. Then he turned and walked quickly away, disappearing down the trail. Callie let out a breath.

"What was that all about?" Melissa asked. "What were you looking at?"

"I'm not sure," Callie said. She stared in the direction Michael had gone. Melissa followed her gaze, but Callie didn't say anything more.

Finally Callie helped Melissa dismount. Melissa petted Star's neck, thanked her for the ride, and crawled back beneath the overhang. Callie followed her.

Melissa lay down and stared at the ceiling thoughtfully. Amy was curled up on the floor; Callie couldn't tell whether she was really sleeping or not.

Callie still wanted to ride Star herself. She crawled back outside.

Star was gone. Callie saw hoofprints along

the trail, but they disappeared after only a few steps. Star had gone in the same direction as Michael. Callie should have guessed Star and Michael would leave together, just as they had before.

Callie sighed, wondering if she'd ever see Star again. She knew she'd been lucky to see her even this once. She looked down the trail, hoping to catch some sign of the horse, a glimpse of hoof or tail.

Instead she saw lights. She heard voices calling out to her.

It was the search-and-rescue team, coming at last to take them out of the mountains.

Chapter Twelve

The rescue workers carried Melissa out on a stretcher; Callie and Amy followed on foot. Josh was with them. He claimed he knew the girls would have made it to the overhang and gotten through the storm all right. He looked so relieved to see them for himself, though, that Callie wasn't sure she believed him.

Callie and Amy told him they'd walked to the overhang, with Melissa leaning on them the whole way. They said they'd started as soon as they'd seen the storm coming in and had taken it slowly. Josh seemed to believe them. He never thought to look down, where Star's hoofprints were still fresh in the mud.

The other horses were okay. Josh had found Rusty, Tiny, and Butterscotch about a mile from the stables, following the trail toward home. The rescue workers had found Pepper on the way back in. The mare was tired and wet but otherwise all right. Someone had already gone on ahead to take her back to the stables.

Josh had told his boss that he thought the

rattlesnake on the trail was what had scared the horses. His boss had accepted that. Josh himself still wasn't convinced, but he couldn't think of a better explanation.

Apparently Callie's parents hadn't been convinced, either; Josh said they were furious with him for losing the horses and leaving the girls in the mountains, even though he'd had no choice but to go for help. "I don't think I've ever heard anyone yell so loud," Josh admitted, wincing. "My ears are still ringing."

Callie had expected the searchers to come with horses or maybe even helicopters, but they apparently operated on foot more often than not. Walking out of the mountains took longer than riding in, and the stretcher slowed them down further. They also had to take detours at times, when too much water blocked the trail. Water was everywhere. The rain had filled all the dry desert washes and gullies, turning them into the rivers they really were.

Patches of clouds drifted away as they walked. The stars came out, glittering against the black sky. Away from the city lights, the stars were all different sizes and colors. The moon grew huge as it neared the horizon. Callie kept looking up as she walked. She wondered whether Melissa found magic in these lights, too.

The sun rose as they neared the bottom of the trail. The sky turned deep blue, with no hint that clouds had ever been there at all. The ocotillo, which had been lifeless gray sticks on the way in, were now covered with the beginnings of tiny green leaves.

Callie's feet hurt. She decided she definitely preferred riding to hiking.

Mom and Dad met the girls at the stables. They'd waited there all night. They hugged Callie and Melissa over and over again, as if unable to believe they really were okay. "We're fine," Callie told them, but they didn't seem to hear her.

Mom rode with Melissa in the ambulance to the hospital. Callie and Dad followed by car. By the time they arrived, the hospital had already confirmed that Melissa's ankle really was only badly sprained, not broken. The doctor gave Mom and Dad some painkillers for her and said she should stay off her feet for a few days.

When Callie told the doctor how cold and clammy Melissa had been, the doctor said Melissa had probably had mild hypothermia, which meant her body temperature had dropped lower than it should have. That could have been much more serious than a sprained ankle, but Callie and Amy had done the right thing by following their instincts and keeping her warm.

"I never want to go through anything like that again," Melissa said, sitting up in the emergency-room bed.

Mom hugged her. "You won't have to, honey. I don't think you'll be riding again for a very long time." She glanced at Dad, as if they'd been discussing something. "I don't think either of you will."

"Mom!" Callie's stomach sank. She'd been through this with her parents once before. They couldn't stop her from riding again. Callie opened her mouth, wondering how to change their minds.

Before Callie could say anything, Melissa spoke. "I want to ride," she said.

Callie stared at her sister, stunned. "But I thought you hated horses," she blurted. Then she put her hand over her mouth; she didn't want to stop Melissa from arguing in her favor, after all.

"I do hate them," Melissa said. "But I'm also sick and tired of being scared of them."

For the first time, Callie was almost impressed by Melissa. Mom just shook her head, though. "Not after the way those horses threw you girls," she said. Her face turned dark. "You don't know how frightened we were, with the way it rained last night, and all that lightning. . . ." Her voice trailed off.

"We were worried about a lot more than whether or not your ankle was broken," Dad said.

Melissa rolled her eyes, then looked at Callie. Callie realized that Melissa thought their parents were being unfair, too. But Callie knew the determined look on their parents' faces all too well. Neither of the girls had any chance of changing their minds.

Not alone, anyway. Maybe if Callie helped Melissa out, together they could convince them. It was worth a try. Callie glanced at Melissa. Melissa returned the look, and together they turned to their parents.

"If we just stick to lessons for a while," Callie said slowly, "we won't be riding at night or in the rain. We'll be right here at the stables."

"You can even come and watch us," Melissa said. "It'll be perfectly safe."

The look on Dad's face softened just a little. Not nearly enough, though.

"Besides," Melissa said, "Callie's already had so many lessons, and I haven't had any at all. It isn't fair."

"And we can help more with the yard if you want," Callie offered. She searched desperately for something they could do. "We'll dig out the pool."

"We will?" Melissa said. She glanced at Callie.

For the first time, Dad smiled. "I don't expect you girls to dig out an entire pool," he said.

"But you'll let us ride?" Callie said.

Dad rubbed at the stubble on his chin. He looked at Mom; Mom looked back at him. For a long time both parents were silent.

"We'll see," Dad said at last. "It's been a long night, and I think we all need some sleep. We can talk about riding lessons later."

Callie fought back a smile. When Dad said "we'll see" about something, he usually agreed, sooner or later. Sometimes it took a while, but chances were that eventually he'd let her ride. That he'd let them both ride.

Callie looked at her sister. Melissa looked back, and Callie saw that her sister also was trying not to smile. Without warning, both girls started laughing. The tension of the long night drained away. They were out of the storm, and they were all right. Right then, that was all that mattered.

The day after they returned home, Callie and Amy sat in Callie's bedroom, an open book by Amy's side, a large glass of iced tea by Callie's. Callie told Amy about Melissa's ride, as well as about discovering that Michael was the one following them.

Outside, Callie heard running water. The storm had turned the wash in her yard into a roaring river. Over the mountains, clouds were gathering again. There would be another monsoon that afternoon. Already the air held the scent of wet dust.

"I think you were right to let Melissa ride,"

Amy said. She smiled. "You know, in person Star is even more beautiful than I'd imagined." Callie knew what Amy was going to say next. "Do you think I could ride her one day?" Amy asked.

"I don't know," Callie said. She walked to the window and stared at the clouds piled over the mountains. "I don't even know if Star will ever come back here again."

That night Callie fell asleep to the rumble of thunder and the sound of rain lashing against her window. She woke to a cold chill down her back and the sound of someone moving around her room. She bolted upright in bed.

Michael sat stiffly in her chair, watching her in the dark. He still seemed a little bit silvery and unreal, but he was more solid than he'd been in the woods. Callie jumped to her feet. What was he doing in her room? How long had he been there? She flipped on the light.

"Hello," Michael said. He wore the same jeans, work shirt, and hat that he always did. Callie felt suddenly embarrassed in her summer nightgown and bare feet.

Michael stood, looking as awkward as she felt. He didn't seem angry at all now, but he did still look confused. Callie wished he would leave. He had no right to be in her room. She wasn't sure

133

she dared ask him to go, though. What if he got angrier than before? She didn't know what happened when ghosts got really mad.

Besides, the room had once belonged to Michael. Callie wasn't sure that gave him the right to be there, but she didn't say anything. Instead she stood there watching him, wondering what he wanted. Did the room look strange to him now, with its recently painted white walls and new gray carpet?

Michael began to walk slowly around the room, touching Callie's furniture, the stuffed animals on her dresser, the edge of her windowsill. That made Callie even more uncomfortable, and she was about to tell him to cut it out when he stopped by the window and stared out into the yard for a while. Was he looking for Star, the way Callie had so many nights?

Michael turned from the window and kept walking. Callie followed him. In the corner of the room he stopped in front of a battered old trunk. The trunk had been his once; it was one of many things his mother, Mrs. Hansen, had left behind when she'd sold the house. Michael knelt beside the trunk and slowly undid the latch. The lid creaked open.

The trunk held Star's saddle. Callie had insisted on keeping it in her room, even though her parents had moved everything else that used to be Michael's out to the garage.

Michael ran his hand reverently along the old leather. "It's still here," he whispered. "Why?"

Callie shrugged. "Your mom kept it," she said. "When she moved away, I kept it, too."

A bitter look crossed Michael's face. "I would have expected Ma to sell the saddle first chance she got," he said. "She always hated Star. Star and me both."

"No, she didn't," Callie said.

Michael stood and turned to face her. "How would you know?" he said.

"If your mom hated you, why'd she save your stuff for so long?" Callie asked. "When I moved in, just about everything you'd ever owned was still in this room. Can't you tell why?"

Michael just looked at her. He really didn't know. Of course, Callie hadn't known why at first, either, but eventually she'd figured it out. She'd practically heard Michael's mother say it herself, in Callie's dreams.

"Your mom still misses you," Callie told him.

A strange, unreadable look crossed Michael's face. For a moment Callie thought he was going to cry, but he didn't. Instead he asked, very quietly, "So why did you keep the saddle?"

"Because it belonged to Star," Callie said.

Michael shook his head. "You keep saying you care about Star so much. But you let that other girl ride her. That doesn't make any sense. Weren't you scared Star wouldn't come back to you?"

"No," Callie said. She'd been uncomfortable sharing Star with Melissa, but she'd never worried that Star would like Melissa more. Star loved her. Callie knew that.

Michael brushed his hair out of his eyes. He squinted at Callie. "Who are you?" he asked at last. "Why do you keep taking Star away?"

"Stop saying that," Callie snapped. "I've never taken Star away. Except for that one ride into the mountains, I haven't seen Star at all for the past month."

Michael seemed confused again. "But she's been with you. Every night you've dreamed about her, she's been in the yard, watching. If it weren't for me, she probably would have walked right up to your window and asked to ride dozens of times. I could barely hold her back. And when she followed you into the mountains, I couldn't stop her at all."

"You held Star back?" Callie stared at Michael, unable to believe his words. She thought of all the dreams she'd woken up from, only to find the yard empty. She thought of how desperately she'd missed Star. "How could you do that? You have no right—"

"She's my horse," Michael said, as if that justified everything.

Anger blurred Callie's sight. She whirled

away from him. She was afraid that if she looked at him one moment more, she'd start yelling, and she didn't want to wake anyone up. She walked over to the dresser and gripped the edge of it so fiercely her knuckles turned white. "I wish I'd never brought Star back to you," she whispered. "I wish I'd just left you alone in the mountains."

"You didn't bring Star back," Michael said. He sounded very sure. "She came on her own. I knew she would."

"I helped her," Callie said. She swallowed back tears. "Don't you know that? Don't you know *anything?*"

Michael didn't answer. Callie was suddenly so tired of talking to him. "Just get out of my room," she said. She turned slowly back around, hoping he'd already be gone.

He still stood there, though, staring at her. His face was puffy, as if he'd cried after all, but his voice was steady enough. "Did you really bring Star back?" he asked.

Callie scowled. "I said I did. It's not the sort of thing I'd make up, you know."

"No," Michael said, his voice very low, "I don't suppose it is." He took a deep breath. "But Star and I were apart for so long. When she followed you into the mountains, I thought I was going to lose her again—this time to you."

"But Star wouldn't leave you," Callie said. Why did Michael have so much trouble understanding that? He was Star's real owner. He and Star belonged together. Their bond was different from Callie's bond to Star, and stronger. Callie had accepted that when Star left the first time.

She expected Michael to argue some more, but instead he just nodded. "I think I'm beginning to see that," he said quietly. He smiled; the expression was strangely sad. "What's your name?" he asked.

"Callie," she said, surprised at the question. She'd known about Michael for a long time now, through Star. Michael seemed to know much less about her, though. "I'm Callie."

Michael walked over to her. "Thank you, Callie, for helping me and Star." He reached out his hand. Startled, Callie shook it. His touch felt every bit as real as Star's did, but colder. It was suddenly hard to believe he was a ghost.

Without another word he turned away from her. He started across the room, toward the door. Before he was halfway there, he began to shimmer. He walked right through her door, disappearing into the hall. Behind him, the room felt suddenly warm.

"Wait!" Callie called. She ran across the room. Michael had asked her so many questions; she suddenly wanted to ask him a few of her own. Like what it was like to be a ghost and why he still was one. Like how he could shimmer and walk through walls like that. A ghost horse—even one as wonderful as Star— couldn't answer those questions. A ghost human could. Callie opened the door and stepped after him, into the hall.

He was gone. The house was silent and still. Callie sighed.

As if in response, she felt something, a familiar tingling running up and down her spine. Callie caught her breath. Michael really had understood. He wasn't holding Star back from her, not anymore. The tingling grew stronger.

Star was outside, waiting for her.

Phantom Rider Rides Again!

GHOST VISION

Phantom Rider

by Janni Lee Simner

Callie knows she's the only person who can see Star. But lately the ghost horse has been appearing at odd times and in strange places—like in front of Callie's school. And Star is starting to look sick. Can Callie find a way to help Star before she fades away forever?

Appearing soon at a bookstore near you.

PR